Nia Bluu

&

The Great Awakening

ALSO, BY MOE NICOLE

They Never Told, But Still Needed You

Live out Loud: Following your purpose even when it's hard

A Fictional Magical Suspense Novel

Nia Bluu

&

The Great Awakening

Written by:

Moe Nicole

*M*oe
*N*icole

AUTHOR.ENTREPRENEUR.CONTENT CURATOR

This book is a work of fiction.

Published by *Live out Loud Press*
An Imprint of Moe Nicole

Manufactured in the United States of America

For information about reproduction or bulk purchasing, please
contact Moe Nicole:
info@moenicole.com

Library of Congress: 2021904879

ISBN-13: 978-1-7340606-2-1
www.MoeNicole.com

To all the outcasts
who never felt like they fit in
traditional society;
This is a safe space for you.

CHAPTERS

ONE

New year, who this?...... 1

TWO

Everything's coming together...... 15

THREE

When it falls apart...... 37

FOUR

The Portal...... 62

FIVE

The Visit...... 90

SIX

The Dream......113

SEVEN

The Soul of the World...... 130

Nia Bluu

&

The Great Awakening

~1~

New Year, Who This?

*As Nikki drove the long stretch home, she looked up into the changing sky that was just the color of the ocean. Right in front of her eyes, it began to spin so fast that she couldn't follow it's direction as the colors swapped from blue, red, purple, and green. As she fixated her eyes on this riveting opening in the sky, she started losing control of her car and then **BOOM**!*

It wasn't even 3pm yet and Nikki found herself daydreaming and tired from all the work she had been doing since six that morning. She finished wrapping up emails, working on her website, and schoolwork; leaving her to question what she would do next. The day had been busy, but she liked it that way.

As she walked from the couch, where she found herself most of the time working, she looked out the window briefly. Within that glance, all she could think about was her 32nd birthday trip. She was planning a trip to Puerto Rico to bring in her birthday, on an ocean-front patio. A trip she had been thinking about since the new year.

She made her way into the kitchen, grabbed a bag of dozitas, and went back to the couch. This year, she was planning a solo birthday trip. This was a trip she had been wanting to take since she saw the show, *She's Gotta Mean It*. As soon as she saw the episode showcasing the main character, Trixa, in Puerto Rico; She booked her flight, a whole 8 months prior.

It was so beautiful to see a black woman exploring a new land and meeting new people that looked just like her. This was something that Nikki found herself desiring to do the older she got. She didn't realize that Puerto Rico had dark-skinned people until she saw that episode. Growing up, Nikki hadn't learned a lot about her family history or their connection to other countries with Black people.

After Nikki made it back to the couch, she picked up her remote to see if there was a new upload on Flixzit she could watch. She hadn't uploaded a video to Flixzit for a while because she needed a break from the everyday hustle of being a creator. Posting consistently was sometimes stressful for her, especially when she was working to become monetized.

Even though she hadn't been uploading any content, recently, that didn't take away from her watching it. So, that's what Nikki decided to do for her break. As soon as she opened the app, she noticed that Yonnie had uploaded a video 1-hour prior. Of course, this excited her, being that Yonnie was one of her favorite Flixziters- Partly because of the content she posted, the other half because of her personality.

Plopped on the couch, Nikki crossed her legs and started watching the video. The title of it was, *Why I'm going celibate and breaking curses.*

Now, that was the type of topic right up Nikki's alley. She had been celibate for about four months after ending things with her on and off again sex-buddy. She got tired of just having a physical relationship with someone and wanted something stronger to build with. For some reason, the men who seemed to be attracted to her had a hard time with commitment. Not only that, but she also had a hard time controlling when she wanted sex, whenever she was sexually active. That desire always seemed to put her in a bad situation, which is why she went celibate.

Nikki already knew this was going to be a good video. As she listened to Yonnie share her reasons for choosing to not date or have sex, she got really intrigued with what Yonnie had to say. She was talking about the relationship she had with her family growing up, more specifically the women in her family.

As the video continued on, she started talking about generational curses. Nikki had heard that term before but never took the time to learn what generational curses actually meant. Yonnie was doing a good job of explaining it, because Nikki found herself beginning to mentally analyze her personal relationships.

As Nikki listened to Yonnie talk about the relationship between her and her grandmother, she was all in. Yonnie explained that many black women tend to have estranged relationships with either their mothers or grandmothers. Those strained relationships oftentimes moved into the type of relationships they had with other people, according to her.

Nikki was in amazement listening to the video, because she had recently been wanting to isolate away from people to reassess who she allowed around her. Lately, she felt like there were a lot of people around that weren't really real, carrying fake energy. The more she thought about it, she became baffled at how it wasn't even just friends. Family had the ability to act just like an enemy.

It was something about Yonnie that drew Nikki to her, especially after her book *Live out Loud*. She had no problem with calling out societal problems to the surface and that book started Nikki's process to living freely.

After that book, Nikki had begun to be more comfortable with her personal experiences and desires in love, life, and purpose. She was no longer holding herself hostage to her personal desires and fears of expressing herself because of how others viewed it.

Thankfully, Nikki made it to a place where she was comfortable with sharing that she liked sex. She was tired of stunting her own self-growth by not fully embracing her sexual side because she was so ashamed of it.

It's definitely the mantra of *Living out Loud* for her now though! Nikki was finally in a free expressive place to just share her story and be an open book, which was why she started her own Flixzit page, showcasing her life. Her page eventually became a large source of income for her, after a year of consistent work.

As Yonnie wrapped up her video, Nikki started leaning back on the couch further and further. All the talk about sex, celibacy, and finding yourself encouraged Nikki to start touching herself in a sensual way. As she wrapped her hands around her neck, she started moving them slowly down until she was cupping her breasts.

She reached over and took a couple puffs from the bong on the table, that still had some weed in it. All it took was one hit of it, for her to sink her head into the arm of the couch and doze off into a deep sleep.

Sinking deep into the dream state, Nikki was walking down a long dark tunnel, towards a light.

While going down the hall there was an eerie energy surrounding her as she looked around. Although the hallway was pitch black, there was a damp smell that made her nostrils cringe with each breath as she walked toward the light at the end of the tunnel. The more she walked, the further the light seemed to be. When she got further down, she heard footsteps approaching her from behind, which made her start running until she tripped over a large object and bumped her head on something sharp.

Nikki woke up soaked in sweat while gasping for air to breathe. *Now my head hurts*, Nikki thought to herself. Yawning with her arms outstretched, she looked over at the clock on the wall. Almost four hours had passed since she had laid down. Nikki already knew that this was a strong indication that it would be hard for her to go back to sleep.

Now what am I going to get into now? Nikki asked herself as she reached for her phone on the table to open up Flixzit. When she looked down at her notifications, she noticed there was a text message from her niece, from an hour prior, telling her that she loved her. That made Nikki's heart smile.

She hadn't seen her nieces and nephews since the last time she was home, one year prior. After that visit, she hadn't been able to travel back home and started to feel disconnected from her family. She talked to her Bibi more than anyone else. Her family loved gossip and making people feel bad, this made Nikki feel like she never fit in since she was a young child.

Nikki started thinking about the dream she had while taking a nap. For some reason she had been having the same dream for a week straight. Every night, she was walking down a dark tunnel towards a bright light. In the dream, she is always unable to see anything, she hardly hears anything, and it always felt like someone was watching her. The dreams always seemed to end with her tripping over a sharp object and waking up with a slight headache.

While thinking about her dream, she looked over at the window in the kitchen and realized she didn't close it. As she got up to go close the window, she remembered she forgot to text her niece back, so she grabbed her phone and took it with her.

When she made it in the kitchen, she realized she hadn't eaten dinner. Nikki started looking through cabinets to find something to prepare for dinner. This was the second day in a row that she didn't have a taste for anything. Knowing that she needed to eat, seemingly irritated her even more, as she opened and closed cabinets before making her way to the refrigerator.

I need to order some groceries she thought to herself as she looked in the freezer at a pack of salmon and shrimp. There had been talks of people needing to start stocking up on food because of a disease going around. If anything were to happen, she would only have enough food to last her about a week and a half.

Finally deciding what to eat, she pulled out the shrimp, a bag of rice from the cabinet, and the last bit of spinach left in the fridge. Cooking had been Nikki's least favorite thing to do domestically. According to her grandmother, that was exactly why she was going to remain single. At every family gathering, she made it known that no man wanted to be with a woman who didn't cook or clean. Every time the conversation came up, Nikki just simply replied, "who needs to know how to cook and clean if you can afford someone to do it for you?" and walked away.

One thing about Nikki's family, on both sides, they loved to talk about people and what they were doing with their life. For this reason, Nikki stayed away in her own bubble. As a new full-time entrepreneur, the last thing she wanted was people around her who were negative. As long as she had something that she could put in her belly, that's all that mattered to her at the end of the day.

Nikki pulled out a skillet and a pot from under the sink, to start preparing her food. She went over to the sink to add water to the pot for her rice, placed it on the stove and lit it up. The stovetop clicked 4 times before the flame appeared. After pouring the rice into the pot, she started seasoning her shrimp, to sauté.

It took Nikki about 20 minutes to finish preparing dinner, which allowed her the opportunity to listen and dance to about five songs. Which was one of her favorite things to do. Every day, she had a solo dance party in her living room or kitchen where she just danced and sang to some of her favorite music. It was something about music and dancing that always made her feel better.

Before heading back to the couch, Nikki reached down to refill Reese's food bowl. For some reason his appetite had increased, and he had been eating and drinking much more. As Nikki's appetite decreased, his increased. Maybe he was stressed just like her. As soon as the food hit the bowl, Reese came running from the back of the apartment barking excitedly.

As Nikki made her way back to the couch with her food, she started thinking about how stressed out she had been the last few months. It was her hope that 2020 would be better, but it was only 2-weeks into the year, and she had a feeling it was going to be a repeat of the year prior.

I can't wait until my trip, Nikki thought to herself as she plopped down on the couch and crossed her legs. *I need to get my housing scheduled as soon as possible for Puerto Rico*, she thought.

Nikki knew, if she didn't find housing soon, she would be left with housing options that would be less desirable. The types that were very sketchy, to be exact! She wasn't looking for much with her housing, outside of wanting an oceanfront apartment with a balcony.

"Katrina, remind me to purchase my housing tomorrow at 6pm!" Nikki yelled out loud to her electronic personal virtual assistant, on the wall.

"I'll remind you tomorrow at 6pm," Katrina responded back.

Placing her food on the coffee table, Nikki picked up her phone and opened Flixzit to find something to watch. As she was scrolling through her timeline feed, she stumbled across a suggested video about the new deadly disease that had been spreading rapidly in the country.

Here comes the bullshit, Nikki thought after reading the title.

There had been a lot of talk on the news that the country was going to be shutting down because of a disease that was going around, called Kurlona or something like that. Although she didn't have cable

TV, Nikki was able to get her news from Flixzit without having too much distraction from the media.

A year ago, last December, Nikki made the decision to stop watching TV and using her LookBook social media page. She found herself spending countless hours on LookBook, and watching TV, doing things that weren't lucrative to her business and growth as a woman.

She'd never been the type to engage in other people's drama online, which is why she could never engage with the big drama TV shows. She had enough theatrics in her life, to the point where she didn't need to be reminded of what she was trying to heal. Especially relationships that ended the year prior. It was after her break-up with Cornell, that she made the decision to give up her page.

The whole situation with Cornell was a lot. On top of that, he was a stubborn Taurus. He wasn't all bad though. Cornell had a way with speaking to Nikki's inner child, but that was about it. He was beyond secretive to the point where he even refused to share his social media handle with her, out of fear she would find and follow him. On top of that, the sex wasn't even good.

He was the living proof that size didn't matter when it came to pleasure, because he had the length, but the stroke was off. Every time they'd have sex, he'd be spitting all over her lady parts and stroking like he was in the middle of a porn scene. That wasn't it!

By this time, she was eating her food while scrolling through Flixzit.

Let me stop thinking about my exes, because they are that for a reason Nikki thought while stumbling upon something to watch.

"Ohhhh this looks interesting!" she said as she saw a new upload from Cindy&Friends.

Cindy was talking about creating the life you want to live and ignoring other people's opinion of you. This was right up Nikki's alley, she had always loved finding new ways to level herself up mentally, emotionally, and physically. Especially going into this new year of life. She was turning 32 and 32 was a really big number for her. Not only had it always been her favorite number, but she read somewhere that the number 32 was really important in a person's life.

Everywhere Nikki looked, there was a columnist writing about how numbers have significant meanings, especially the number 32. Nikki's life path number was 5, and the number 32 is deduced to be the number 5, which meant that was the year that she was supposed to come into her true self and power according to the astrologist and numerologists. Needless to say, she took the information loosely.

"Helloooooo my beautiful unicorn friends, welcome back to Cindy&Friends!" Cindy chimed in enthusiastically on her video. "Today, we are going to talk about walking in your purpose, grab your food, grab your drink, and let's have girl talk!" She added.

"I'm one step ahead of you CinCin!" Nikki responded out loud, before realizing she hadn't grabbed anything to drink with her food. She slid off the couch to get bottled water from the kitchen. As she walked to the kitchen a cold drift of air blew through the house sending a cool sensation through her body from her feet up. She looked at her door to see if she left it open, which she hadn't. She looked over at the window she closed earlier, and it was closed too. She simply shrugged and kept on.

She grabbed a bottled water from the floor, next to the refrigerator, and made her way back to the couch, forgetting about the cold drift of air that just passed through her home.

Nikki sat on the couch and enjoyed her meal while listening to CinCin share her perception of manifestation on the screen. As she was explaining the law of attraction, her eyes were twinkling like little stars lighting up the sky as her hair bounced up and down while she excitedly shared her experience.

Once the video wrapped up, Nikki went to the kitchen to wash her dishes. When she finished, she dried her hands on the towel and made her way to the bathroom to shower. As Nikki walked in the bathroom, she took a long look into the mirror. Her locs hung past her shoulders, with colorful ends resembling a fresh rainbow. Her caramel-colored skin was full of acne spanning from one cheek to the other.

It took Nikki a long time to come to loving herself flaws and all. She used to complain about her eyebrows being too wild, her lips not being plump, and her bad eyesight through almond shaped pupils. As she took her purple butterfly-shaped glasses off to prepare for her shower, everything became blurry and the flaws of her body were no longer of importance.

When Nikki finished showering, she made her way to the kitchen to grab water before bed. While drinking her water, she looked over at the window next to the sink and noticed that it was open again. This was the same window she closed earlier. As she started closing the window, she saw a black cat sitting outside her window. The cat was staring at her, until Nikki finished closing the window and left the kitchen. She simply assumed she didn't close it completely earlier and made her way to the bedroom.

~2~

Everything's coming together

As the clouds started rising with the sun, the crisp morning air blew against the window sounding like it was singing a good morning song. It was a few minutes before 6am and Nikki found herself rolling over to face the sun awakening alongside her.

No matter the time she went to sleep, her body had gotten used to waking up with the sun. So just like clockwork she was rolling over to begin another day.

You'd think she'd be used to her mornings starting that way, but it was still a shocking surprise everytime her body woke up. Nikki let out a deep sigh, as she rolled over to get out the bed.

Nikki swung her feet across the edge of the bed, letting her legs dangle off the sides. While wiping her eyes, she stood up and bent her back as far as she could in an effort to stretch out the bedtime paralysis that had taken over her limbs. After gaining her composure, she slipped her feet into the slippers sitting on the floor next to the head of her bed and made way to the bathroom.

What do I have to do today? She asked herself, as she added items to the do-list in her head.

sssssssss *went the sound of her pee hitting the toilet bowl*, as she sat on the seat and began relieving herself.

Nikki started feeling good as she relieved herself. As her eyes started rolling in the back of her head, she realized she hadn't said her morning prayers and what she was grateful for to the creator.

She found herself going deeper into her subconscious to ask herself, *What am I thankful for today?*

She started saying out loud the things she was thankful for. Every day it was something different, but that day, she wanted to say thank you for the simple things in life. She had her necessities, resilience, and a roof over her head; There was nothing to complain about.

Nikki leaned forward while she wiped herself from front to back before flushing the toilet. She immediately jumped up, washed her hands and returned to her room to grab her robe. Surprisingly, Reese was nowhere to be found, which meant he was still somewhere asleep.

"Reese!" Nikki yelled out. "Let's go outside!"

Reese peeked his head out from under the couch in Nikki's living room. Creeping slowly, he stretched his right leg out and then his left leg while letting out a big yawn. Once he finished stretching, he shook his body and ran to the back door.

"Sit," Nikki said softly, while motioning her hand over his head. Reese sat gracefully, as she reached for the leash to attach to his collar. After hooking it up, she opened the door to a nice crisp temperature. She saw each car had a frost over its windows which made her shiver from her belly to her chest. Nikki let Reese run out the door and closed the screen door while he ventured around the backyard to do his business.

As she watched him walk around the backyard, she noticed a black cat sitting on the porch of a neighbor's apartment. As the cat was sitting on the porch watching Reese, she turned to look at Nikki abruptly. Her eyes were the color yellow- a bright yellow with rays that shimmered like gold reflecting the sun. Nikki looked at the cat in amazement of the feline's unusual beauty and light ray brightened eyes. She had just seen a black cat the night before, but their eyes were nowhere near as beautiful.

Something is not normal about that cat, Nikki thought to herself as she opened the door for Reese to come back inside. While still looking at the cat, Nikki shook her head and mumbled, "something isn't right," and closed the door behind Reese before locking it.

"Sit," Nikki prompted Reese, while closing the door. Reese was already sitting and waiting for her to remove his leash from his collar. After 9 years of the same routine, Reese had become very accustomed to the repetition of his outside routine, to the point where he knew what to do before being instructed. After getting his leash off, he ran to his water bowl and started drinking as if he hadn't had water in 2 weeks.

Nikki placed the leash on the table next to the couch and went to the bathroom to start getting ready for the day.

She couldn't wait until she got a husband who liked to cook, because it would be perfect to have breakfast ready by the time she got out the bathroom. She walked in the bathroom and turned on the light before looking in the mirror and reading the affirmations written across the top with lipstick. This was suggested by one of her online friends, who was big on the law of attraction and manifestation. Still confused on how much it actually worked, Nikki read them every morning to get her day going, it made her feel good in the moment to start the day off.

She walked over to the tub and turned on the water. With her hands under the running water, she waited until the temperature was perfect to the touch before removing her hand from under the faucet. She stood up, while pulling the shower curtains across, and started removing her clothes.

Starting with her robe, she undressed until she was naked, standing in the mirror. Something about seeing herself in the mirror turned her on and made her start touching her neck with one hand on each side. While rolling her head around in a circle, she ran her hands down her body, stopping at her chest. With each hand cupping a breast, she massaged each one gently. The warm and soft feel of her breasts brought a sensation that made her roll her head backwards in comfort, as she exhaled.

Nikki moved her fingertips slowly towards her nipples and pinched them until the sharp shocking sensation traveled through her entire body. Still pinching her left nipple, her right hand moved slowly down to her lady parts. She let out a deep sigh as he looked in the mirror again. At this point she was massaging inside her lady parts and rubbing her middle finger inside her juicy and wet vagina while her index finger massaged her clit.

Who really needs a man for an orgasm, when I can give it to myself? She asked herself jokingly while walking toward the shower and stepping in.

Nikki started thinking about the last time she had sex with someone. It was hard to remember all the moments of the last time she was in the presence of masculine energy to bounce ideas off. It had been months since she had been with a man, but she didn't have the desire to be with one either. It had become easier for her to say no to anyone who didn't give her a good vibe.

As she got into the shower, Nikki took her scrubby and soaked it in preparation for the soap. There were so many things she wanted to do, sexually, but she wanted to do it with someone who was long-term. Until then, she would continue to explore her body alone.

Although Nikki enjoyed being single, she questioned if it was fair to hold herself back sexually, in hopes of finding a mate. What if she never found one? So many thoughts ran through her mind as she cleaned off her body in the shower, from her toes to her neck.

Before stepping out, she reached for her towel to start drying off. After drying off, she wrapped the towel around her body, tucked it in, and stepped out the shower. She grabbed her toothbrush from the blue holder on the right side of the sink, placed it under the automatic toothpaste dispenser, and put a little water on it before brushing her teeth.

While brushing her teeth, she started thinking about what she needed to do for the day.

Nikki immediately began making a mental list of everything she needed to get done for the day. She had to schedule her blog posts, script her upcoming Flixzit videos, and call her grandma. Instead of attempting to remember everything, she commanded her virtual home assistant to remind her.

"Katrina!" She yelled to her virtual home assistant, "Create a list for the day."

Katrina responded back, "Creating a list for the day, what would you like to name this list?"

"You can name it tasks for Monday the 6th," Nikki said.

"List Monday the 6th has been created; would you like to begin adding items to this list?"

"Yes," she responded, taking a moment to think about what she needed to add before listing them out.

Nikki was known for forgetting things, which is why she had a deep feeling that she was forgetting something. This prompted her to go write it down once more when she finished brushing her teeth.

What she needed to do, honestly, was get a healthy schedule and routine together to where she had her day planned out the day before. This was a recurring thought of Nikki's, as it crossed her mind once more while she looked for her notebook. Maybe then, she wouldn't have to worry about forgetting something or ignoring something that needed to get done. If she planned the night before and remembered something else the next day; it made the day more complete.

In that moment, Nikki remembered that she needed to schedule a reminder for her to purchase housing for her birthday trip.

"Katrina, add find housing for Puerto Rico to my list Monday the 6th," Nikki shouted at her virtual home assistant.

"Adding find housing for Puerto Rico to your list Monday the 6th," Katrina responded back.

"Thank you Pooh!" Nikki responded back.

I don't know why I talk back to her like she is a real person Nikki thought to herself while giggling at the thought.

As she thought about it, it was smarter to call her grandma while doing her makeup. She would be able to hit two birds with one stone and be smarter with her time since it was such a long day ahead.

Nikki walked into the second room, grabbed her makeup chair, and moved it into the bathroom for her to sit on. She then grabbed her phone from the living room and walked back to the bathroom to prepare.

After taking a seat in the chair, Nikki yelled to Katrina, "Katrina, call Grandma A cell."

"Calling Grandma A cell," Katrina responded back.

In a brief moment, Nikki felt a slight guilt for how much she had been depending on technology in her daily life. She couldn't help but to think about how lazy it was making her with simple tasks. *Phone Rings*

"Helllllo," answered Nikki's Grandma.

"Hey Granny, how are you doing?"

"I'm doing alright hunny, how are you doing?" she responded.

"I'm doing good, just starting to get dressed, putting on my makeup. I knew you would be awake with the sun, especially being an hour ahead of me." Nikki said back jokingly.

"You definitely guessed that right! Me and Dad are just sitting here enjoying a cup of coffee looking at the morning news before I head out to town," she responded.

"Oh, you have some clients to see today?" Nikki asked.

"Yeaaaa, one of them fell yesterday because she was so damn hardheaded. We tell her all the time to ring her alarm for help when she wants to get up for something. You can't gain 500 pounds and get mad at everyone else when you can't do it for yourself anymore. Life got that way; you know what I mean?"

"Wooooow 500 pounds, I can only imagine what it took to get that far and how she must be feeling," Nikki responded back.

"I know she misses her independence, but she had to realize certain things are going to be hard for her, so she is going to have to get help until she can do it on her own. When she doesn't, it puts more on me and her daughter because we have to work overtime to not only get her together but, deal with the after-effects of pain management." Nikki's grandmother said with a concerned tone in her voice.

"Oh, I didn't think about that! You have to go through a lot in your field for sure. I don't know how you are still working in the field." Nikki responded with concern.

"I'mma tell you something. When you are doing what you love, it doesn't feel like work and you can find yourself wanting to do it until the day you die," her grandmother responded with pride in her voice. You could tell by her tone that she enjoyed her job.

"Wow, when you put it that way, it makes so much sense." Nikki said.

By this time, she finished shaping her eyebrows and was now working on her eye shadow.

"Yah know, that's why I always told you and your siblings that you have to do what you love, even if someone else doesn't understand it. Including me. I don't want to get in the way of you doing what you love. You have to live with your choices not me, not your mom, not dad: Nobody."

"That's true granny. That's true," Nikki said with her eyes squinted as she added a bright blue to her eyes.

"If you don't take anything else from me, I want you to always know that when you are following what you love, you will be taken care of. You will have everything you need to have. Even when you get stressed out; you will find yourself getting back up on your feet and making it happen. Because when you love it and you have responsibilities to take care of, you make it happen! When I took your siblings in, it was because I loved y'all and I wouldn't be able to live with myself if I didn't take the responsibility," Her grandma responded back.

"You know, y'all came to live with me shortly after me and dad got married."

All of that sacrifice in the midst of a busy life. Nikki's grandmother, Anjelique, was a newlywed when she adopted Nikki's siblings. They had been married for less than a year and she was just starting a graduate school program.

Nikki responded back with a laugh, "That's true! It took me forever to even call him granddad because I was still getting accustomed to him being around you."

"Yea, so a lot changed in a short period of time. But we loved each other so we took on the responsibility of doing what needed to be done while still living our life. It wasn't easy, but it was necessary to be done- And I won't talk about how my sex life died when I took y'all in!" She said with a roaring laugh.

"Granny, I don't want to know anything about you and grandad doing grown-folk stuff," She giggled. "How have you and grandad been outside of work?" Nikki asked while starting to put foundation on her face, with a makeup sponge.

"We've been doing good baby. I don't have anything to complain about. Now, I need for him to not be so hard-headed when I'm trying to help him. Outside of that, we are doing good baby. How are you doing out there?"

Nikki responded, "I'm doing well. I've been thinking about flying back home to see everyone, but I'm trying to figure out when. You know I'm supposed to be going to Puerto Rico in a couple of months for my birthday."

"Ohhhh, I like Puerto Rico. Who are you going with?" She asked.

"I'm going by myself. I was going to go to Belize with a few friends, but I changed my mind and decided to go somewhere alone along the ocean."

"Maybe you'll find your husband down there. You know they like women that look like us," Her Grandmother said in a serious yet joking tone.

27

"Granny, I'm not about to play with you today," she laughed. "I'm going down there to get connected to nature, spend some time with myself and figure out what I want my next steps to be. I feel like I am able to relax and do really good planning when I am near a beach," Nikki admitted.

"I understand baby. But remember, you are over 30 and our family has a long history of early hysterectomies. I don't want you to lose your window of fertility." Her grandmother warned. Nikki felt triggered by the sudden turn in the conversation as she began to contour her face.

"Yea, I understand Granny, I'm just waiting on the perfect person for me to build a family with."

"I know baby, it will come", her grandmother assured her, "I just hope you're not hiding away from the men because Derrick was a good man."

Nikki, beginning to feel where the conversation was going, so she simply responded, "Yea... we wouldn't have been happy long-term though and that's what matters most to me."

There was a brief silence.

"Don't act like you can't hear me. You know I am not meant to be no first lady of anyone's church, Granny."

"God delivers!" she swiftly responded back.

"Ha! Well, it seems like God must've told everyone except me. Maybe, just maybe... I'm a little broken," Nikki chuckled cynically. "Well, I need to go and start getting my day started, I'm going to give you a call back to finish catching up Granny." Nikki said, trying to wrap up the conversation.

"Alright baby, I'll talk to you later. Be careful. You know they are saying there is a deadly airborne disease going around and it's spreading fast," She responded.

"Yea, I heard about it, I've been trying to keep from giving too much energy to it."

"Bye baby," her Grandma said and then the two hung up.

The conversation had Nikki thinking about why she didn't like spending too much time with her family. It's something about being a woman. They have gone through and endured so many things over the course of their lineage. It was when her grandmother started talking about hysterectomies and marriage, that she knew the conversation wasn't going to be lasting that long. Nikki didn't feel like thinking about why she didn't have a man or a baby after the age of 30. She brushed the thought aside and focused on putting on her makeup.

As much as she wanted to get that talk out of her head, she couldn't avoid it. Replaying her grandmother's lines in her mind over and over, she started thinking about her dating life. She wondered why she was still single- right now, she could proudly say that it was by choice, but that didn't stop her from questioning whether or not she would be forever alone.

Nikki stared in the mirror and mimicked her grandmother in a silly way, to try and change the energy. For some reason she thought making a joke about what happened would cause her to forget how she really felt. The same feelings she found herself questioning more often, than not, the older she got. For years she had been testing the theory of happiness, compromise and relationships. For some reason- it seemed like, if she wanted to be happy in a relationship; she would have to settle. She would not be allowed to express her feelings. She wouldn't be allowed to have boundaries or basic expectations, because love was meant to be unconditional right? It was hard for her to prescribe to that notion.

Feeling herself beginning to get slightly irritated, she finished her makeup and started posing in the mirror, with pouty lips.

"Oh, I'm cute!" Nikki said excitedly before sticking her tongue out and posing.

She went to her bedroom, got dressed, and then went into her spare bedroom that she turned into her office space. In this space, she did all of her work. Well, that was the plan. Most days, she found herself sitting across the couch with her laptop in front of her. Over the next 5 hours, Nikki managed to complete most of her work-related tasks and rewarded herself with a well-deserved lunch break.

By the time she finished lunch, she took a seat on the couch and opened her laptop to Rentmeup, an online marketplace that consisted of inexpensive housing for travelers all around the world. By this time, she was ready to book her housing for her trip in March, before the prices doubled. Nikki could just picture the beachside from her balcony.

After about an hour of combing through the site, she bookmarked five homes as her top picks. She decided to stop there and finish later that night. Nikki closed the laptop and placed it on the nearby coffee table and reached for her phone on the couch next to her.

Nikki unlocked her cellphone and opened the Pictuhgram app on her phone. Excited that she had narrowed down the search for housing, she started creating a post for her profile. Of all the pictures she had, she decided on an old picture of her in a bathing suit. She captioned it, *I can't wait to wear this on the beach*, and clicked share. Not even a minute later, someone commented on the picture, "You're not going anywhere with Kurlona spreading like wildfire."

Nikki ignored the comment and closed the application from her phone. She sat the phone on the table and went to the bathroom. As she was walking in the bathroom, she accidentally tripped over Reese, making him whimper loudly and run away.

"I'm so sorry baby!" Nikki said to Reese, although he was nowhere in sight by that time.

Instead of using the bathroom, she went back, grabbed her phone and took it with her. As she sat on the toilet seat, she unlocked her phone and opened the Pictuhgram app to see if she had any comments on her post.

As she looked at the notifications, there were more people telling her not to travel while Kurlona was present. There were also men commenting how beautiful she was. That was nothing new for Nikki though, she was used to having men swarming around her interested- for quite some time. Even if she ignored them, they kept coming back.

While responding to comments, she received a notification of a new message in her inbox. It was from a guy she had been communicating with through direct messages, innocently- but flirtatious at the same time. It was something about the back-and-forth messages that was intriguing to her. He responded to messages, had valuable information to share on questions, and he was very handsome on top of his perceived intelligence. As much as Nikki had been wanting to stay single and not engage with anyone on a romantic level, for some reason she was being drawn to him.

Nikki and this guy had never met in person, but their virtual conversations had become more intriguing over the last couple of weeks. It started with him responding to her post regarding polyamory and women having two men as a mate. Needless to say, he was totally against it, but he provided a great context to the conversation. Their conversations evolved from that message to discussing the media and the state of black people in America.

Let me see what he has to say, Nikki thought to herself as she went to open the message, with a smile on her face. Torine was responding to her last post on her timeline.

"You are fooling Nikki!" He replied.

Nikki took this message as another flirting opportunity and played along with him. She responded back, "What I dooooo?!" with full knowledge of what he was talking about.

As soon as she sent the message, she received a notification that he read it. Either he was reading their old messages, or he clicked the notification as soon as it came through, because it happened quickly. Nikki was anxiously waiting to see what he had to say as she watched the typing bubbles move across the bottom of the screen.

"Now, you know what I'm talking about Nikki! Let's not play confused haha," he typed back.

At this point, Nikki took that as a sign that he was flirting back with her. She decided to keep the conversation going by asking him how his day was going. When Torine typed, "it's actually not going too well..."

Nikki responded, "what's wrong?" With feelings of concern.

"I just have a lot on my mind" Torine responded back quickly.

Nikki started feeling more concerned about what was on his mind and offered to be a listening ear. He told her thank you and left it at that. Nikki's heart started beating fast and the palms of her hands started sweating, as she nervously thought about calling him. They both shared their phone numbers in messenger, but she decided she was going to call him through Pictuhgram instead.

For some reason, Nikki was nervous to call him. A part of her nervousness was because she didn't know if he was going to answer. Another part of her nervousness was because she knew she had an interest in him and she told herself she wouldn't get involved with anyone for the entire year. For unknown reasons, she decided to still give him a call because she wanted to make sure he was ok.

Two rings into the call, Torine answered-"Oh shoot, Ms. Nikki called me! I didn't even know you could do that on this app!"

That's all it took for them to kick off the conversation that ended up lasting until one in the morning. During the conversation, they both talked about what was on their minds, they talked about their backgrounds, what they did for a living, and they even shared their most embarrassing moments in life with each other. It was something about the vibe that led them to talk on the phone every day, for the next two months straight.

During their time connecting with each other, Nikki learned that Torine had just recently got out of a bad relationship and moved into his own place.

They both enjoyed each other's time, even though they were long distance. They spent so much time together that they created a joint morning, midday, and evening routine. This went on for two months before they even got a chance to plan on seeing each other face to face. Their friendship quickly turned into a long-distance relationship that felt like a match made in heaven.

~3~

When it falls apart

Nikki opened her eyes to find herself in a dark tunnel, with only a small glimpse of light peeking through in the distance. She nervously walked toward the light, in hopes of finding the exit from the dark space she had found herself in. As she walked towards the light, it got smaller and smaller until she found herself in a pitch-black space.

The room was dark and cold with a lingering damp smell. Nikki started hyperventilating as her claustrophobia started to trigger from the enclosed space. As the sound of her breathing picked up, she heard a sound behind her. As it got louder, she noticed it was footsteps and started to get nervous.

Out of nowhere, she screamed out, *Reveal yourself!* Not knowing what the response would be, suddenly a bright light lit up the entire space. The light was so bright that Nikki was unable to withstand it. She attempted to place her hand over her eyes and peer in the direction of where the footsteps were, the light had become so bright that her ears started ringing. Unable to withstand the ringing and the brightness, Nikki passed out.

She abruptly woke up and began panting while touching on her body to see if she was awake.

Panicking and breathing heavy, Nikki replayed the dream frantically.

She rolled over to look at the time and realized Torine hadn't called her for their morning talk. He usually called every morning at 8am, and they would start their day with stretches and meditation through video chat. Not thinking anything of it, she rolled over to the side of her bed and picked up her phone to call him instead.

The phone rang about 10 times before going to voicemail, prompting Nikki to end the call. Not thinking anything of it, she swung her legs over the side of the bed and made her way to the bathroom. As she sat on the toilet, she opened her phone to Flixzit and there was a video playing live from the news, titled *"***URGENT: ENTIRE COUNTRY IS ON LOCKDOWN!***"*

Nikki clicked the video, to see the words, "*All stores, airports, and non-medical facilities are closed until further notice due to Kurlona.*" flashing across the bottom of the screen.

Nikki, immediate got upset as she started yelling at the phone while her pee started streaming into the toilet. Her flight was scheduled to leave in three days for Puerto Rico and that was the last thing she wanted to hear.

She immediately closed the application, opened her internet browser, and started searching for more information on the Kurlona shut down. This was the worst time for this to be happening, in her eyes, since it was only a few days before her birthday. She had been looking forward to the trip for such a long time.

Every search result showed the same headline: ALL STORES, AIRPORTS, AND NON-MEDICAL FACILITIES ARE ON LOCKDOWN.

Nikki went to the airline's website and logged into her account. There it was, the headline she had seen on every other website was there as well. It was true, there was no Puerto Rico and there was no birthday trip. An airline notice popped up, that read: *All customers can cancel their trips for a full refund or receive a credit with a bonus 10,000 frequent flyer points on their account.*

Since Nikki was still planning to travel to Puerto Rico, she decided to keep the credit for the extra points; it made more sense to her at the moment.

Nikki thought about how she hadn't talked to Torine and then now she was being forced to cancel her birthday trip. She was frightened to think about what other bad news she could receive before her birthday. She proceeded to log into the Rentmeup website to cancel her housing. Her anger was radiating heat and it could be seen all over her face.

Just as she finished submitting her refund request her phone started ringing. It was her childhood best friend, Nicki with a C. Instead of calling her Nicki, she liked to call her by her middle name, Simone.

"Hey Mone, what's up Pooh?" Nikki answered the phone.

"Hey best friend, how are you doing?" Simone responded abruptly.

"I'm doing good, despite the fact I just had to cancel my birthday trip three days before my plane was supposed to take off." Nikki responded back angrily.

"Awe, I am so sorry best friend, I can only imagine how you feel. I know they put everything on emergency lockdown because a large group of people died this morning from Kurlona. Are you sitting down?" Simone asked.

"Yea, I've been sitting on the toilet for the last 15 minutes trying to figure everything out with my trip." Nikki said with a giggle.

"Ok, I don't know how to say this to you, but I just saw the ambulance outside Bibi's house, so I ran across the street to see if everything was ok..." Simone started speaking.

"What are you about to tell me Simone?" Nikki interrupted her.

"They just rushed Bibi to the hospital in the ambulance," Simone answered with slight hesitation.

"What do you mean by they just rushed Bibi to the hospital? What happened to her? Is she ok? I'm going to need a little more than that," Nikki demanded.

"I don't know best friend. All I know is that I went over there when I saw the lights. Your dad and uncle were over there with the ambulance too. He said he tried to call you, but he couldn't get through, so that's why I called," she responded in a low tone.

Nikki, able to hear the sincere worry in Simone's voice, responded, "Thank you best friend. I appreciate you for calling to let me know. I don't

know why his call didn't come through but I'm glad
that yours did, at least."

"You're welcome best friend," Simone responded.
"If I hear anything before you do, I will let you know.
You should try to call your dad."

"Thank you pooh, I'll keep you updated," Nikki said
while ending the call abruptly. She didn't even wait
for Simone to say goodbye before hanging up. She
quickly dialed her father's phone and he answered on
the first ring.

"Hey baby, did you talk to Simone already?" He
asked.

"Yes, I did, she wasn't able to tell me a lot. What is
going on, do I need to come back home today?"
Nikki asked.

With a slight hesitation, he responded back, "I think
it may be best if you could find a way to get here
safely. I know they just shut down the airports."

"It's ok, I can drive, it's like an 11-hour drive at most.
All I have to do is pack, take a nap and then I will be
on the road by tonight. Do you think she will make it
until I get there early in the morning?" Nikki asked
hastily.

"Just get here safely baby girl, that's all that matters," he responded.

"What do you mean by just get there safely? Will she still be alive?" Nikki asked with a tremble in her voice.

Her dad responded, "Only God knows what will be. Let me know if you need anything or any help getting here. I need to get off the phone and go back in here with the ER doctors, they are trying to explain a bunch of things to us and I can't have my phone in there."

"Ok, I'll let you know when I'm on the way!" Nikki responded back.

They both hung up the phone without saying goodbye. Nikki placed the phone on the bathroom counter and grabbed some toilet paper to wipe herself. As she wiped herself, the tears started flowing down her face. Something in her told her that her Bibi was dead and that she was not going to hear her voice again.

Nikki and her Bibi talked on the phone, the night before, briefly. When Nikki called her, she said she was getting ready to go to bed because she wasn't feeling well and was tired. Before hanging up the phone, she asked Nikki to pray for her. As the tears ran down her face, Nikki pleaded with God to heal Bibi.

While giving herself a pep talk, she started thinking about everything she had to pack before going home. Scrambling to gather herself together, she stood up from the toilet, pulled up her underwear, and walked over to the bathroom sink. As she looked in the mirror, all she saw were tears running down her face wetting the canvas that was smiling just the day before.

She turned on the sink water to wash her hands, but instead of pumping soap into her hands, she decided to throw water on her face. Something about the day didn't feel real. From waking up from such another dark dream, to not hearing from her boyfriend, her trip being cancelled, and now the news of Bibi potentially being at the end of her life; all she could do was wail.

A large part of herself wished she wasn't awake, but reality reminded her that she was. She started wiping her eyes of the water she had thrown on herself just moments prior. While shaking her drying hands, droplets of water hit the sink counter and mirror.

Nikki picked up her phone and called Torine again. The phone rang about 9 times before she hung up and threw it on the floor. Upset, she walked into her office room, opened the closet and grabbed her suitcase from the back. She drug the suitcase from the closet to the bed and slammed it down angrily before unzipping it and starting the packing process.

At this time, Nikki was not only frustrated about what happened with Bibi, she was frustrated with Torine and him not answering her phone calls. Her anger was coming out with each dresser drawer she opened and closed, slamming them each time before throwing the contents onto the bed. *Oh, he got me fucked up,* Nikki thought to herself as she became a raging storm.

ring ring rinnng

Nikki looked over at her phone with a glimpse of hope that it was Torine calling her back, but it wasn't. It was her cousin. She didn't really want to hear anything else bad, so she ignored the call and turned back to her mediocre packing efforts.

She walked over to her dresser and opened the top- middle drawer where her under garments were and threw panties on the bed, like a tornado appeared. It was clear she had no intentions of matching anything nor did she care what type of panties she packed. She was throwing thongs, boy shorts, and period panties on the bed. After the panties, she went for her pants and bottoms. Nikki grabbed 3 pairs of leggings, 2 pairs of jeans, and a dress from her closet and packed them all into the suitcase. The thought of the dress made her break down crying again.

As she took a long gaze at the dress, she decided to put it back on the hanger and in the closet. By bringing the dress, she felt like it was an indication of Bibi dying and she didn't want that implication.

Nikki took the next 30 minutes packing her clothes, shoes, and toiletries into the suitcase. She packed up her laptop, schoolbooks, and food for Reese last. Once she finished, she went to the living room, plopped down on the couch, and pulled out her smoke box to indulge. Nikki opened her smoke box, pulled out her hemp wraps, bag of marijuana, and placed them both on the table. She took out a couple nuggets and started breaking them down on the table before rolling it up.

While smoking, she laid back on the couch and watched the smoke blow out of her mouth and create a cloud. As the smoke disseminated in the air, Nikki slowed her breathing as she exhaled. While taking a deep breath in with the next hit, she closed her eyes and held her breath for 5 seconds before exhaling again. The hemp roll was a little over halfway gone before she put it out and stretched her body across the couch in a rested state.

As Nikki felt herself falling asleep, she knew it was best to set an alarm to be on the road by a certain time. "Katrina, set an alarm for 4pm today," Nikki commanded her virtual home assistant.

"Alarm set for 4pm today," Katrina responded.

Nikki's mind slowly stopped racing as she fell into a deep sleep. The deeper she got into the sleep, the more vivid her dream had become once more; leaving her to find herself back in the same empty dark room as before. Instead of being cold and damp like the last time, it was warm and smelled like freshly cooked dinner. Confused, Nikki decided to just lay on the ground and close her eyes. As she closed her eyes, she heard a voice say softly, "You're almost there. The light isn't too far away."

The vivid dream suddenly stopped, and she drifted into a deep sleep.

A few hours later, Nikki's alarm sounded off, waking her up. She sat up and stretched her arms wide while yawning. While pushing out another yawn, she scratched her head before standing up from the bed. She stopped for a moment and looked around the room before beginning the process of packing everything into her car. After Nikki got everything packed into the car, she went back into the house to grab Reese, her phone, and purse.

As soon as she got into the car, her phone rang, and to her surprise it was Torine. He was finally returning Nikki's phone call, but now Nikki found herself hesitant to answer his call. After the 5th ring, she decided to not answer the phone and placed it in the cup holder as she settled into her seat.

Once she got settled in her seat, she pressed the brake down and pressed the button on her dashboard to start the car. As she shifted the gear from park to drive, she got an alert on her dashboard of a text message from Torine.

Nikki couldn't help but wonder what he wanted, as she found herself getting irritated again. After a few moments, she decided to hear what he had to say. She pressed read on the dashboard and the car started reading Torine's text message.

"Hey Baby, sorry it's been a crazy day from the morning to now, give me a call when you can."

Nikki rolled her eyes as the text message was read out loud. She was going back and forth between if she would believe him or ignore him. After a few moments, she prompted the car to dial his phone number. The phone rang 1 time before Torine answered it with a swift, "Hey Baby," that sounded like he had just finished running up and down the block.

"Hey," Nikki replied back blandly.

"How have you been today? Sorry, I missed your call earlier. I was really busy," Torine responded back.

"Oh man, what happened?" Nikki asked.

"A lot, it's too much and I don't feel like talking about it right now." Torine responded.

"Oh ok," Nikki added with a slight disdain for the direction of the conversation.

"What are you up to? I miss you Baby!" Torine shot back with an elevated pitch and excitement in his voice. It sounded like he was trying to change the energy of the conversation, especially since Nikki's tone wasn't hiding her true feelings in relation to his response.

"I'm just headed back home for some family matters," she responded in monotone.

"You're driving to Michigan right now? What happened with your birthday trip?" Torine asked.

"Well, all of the airports are closed down because of Kurlona and I have a family emergency that I don't feel comfortable speaking about right now," she responded.

Torine, sounding confused, "what do you mean? You usually don't have a problem sharing what's wrong with you."

"The same way you just chose to not disclose why I haven't talked to you all day? Yea, I understand." Nikki snapped. "I'm going to focus on the road, and I'll let you know when I make it."

"Baby, you don't have to be like that. I'm sorry, it's just a lot and I want to listen to you," Torine pleaded with Nikki to keep talking. "I didn't know they shut down the airports today. I'm so sorry you're not able to go on your trip, I know how much you wanted to go."

"Yea, it'll be ok. I have more important things to worry about right now," She responded.

"Are you sure? Do you want me to stay on the phone with you until you make it?" He asked out of worry.

"They rushed my Bibi to the hospital this morning and I'm almost sure she is dead, and I will never get a chance to hear her voice again!" Nikki responded, while pressing on the gas more and more. She started to feel her body temperature rise as tears started swelling up in her eyes.

"You know what, I really don't feel like talking right now. I just want to drive and make it home to see my Bibi. I'll share my location and talk to you later," Nikki finished speaking.

"Ok baby, I understand," Torine responded, realizing he wasn't going to win the battle.

"Bye," Nikki stated bluntly before ending the call. She didn't even wait to see if he was going to respond back. After hanging up the phone, she went to her message settings and shared her location with him.

As she set the phone down in the drink holder, she pressed play on her dashboard and her travel playlist started blaring through the speakers. Hoping to clear her mind, at least for the drive, she started sing along to the lyrics of each song. Some songs were happy, and some were sad. Either way, she was singing them all.

Nikki was so focused on her music and road that she didn't even notice that she had been driving for four hours before stopping. Just as the 4-hour mark hit, her gas light came on. It had gotten dark an hour ago and the next exit was for Mount Verson, Illinois. She was in conservative country, so Nikki decided to wait until the next trucker's stop 10 miles up the road, which was a little more liberal and familiar. Not that she had a problem with conservatives, she just didn't want to stop in an unknown area at nighttime alone.

After her first gas stop, Nikki cruised along and stopped again when she made it to Chicago. She stopped at Winnie's Wings & Tings to grab their famous veggie wings and giblets. She was less than 3 hours away from her hometown, but was getting slightly sleepy, so she decided to grab a coffee from a coffee shop across the street from Winnie's Wings & Tings.

By the time Nikki made it to Chicago, Torine had texted her every 30 minutes to check and see how she was doing on the road, even though he had access to her location. She only responded every hour, and it took a lot for that. For some reason, he rubbed her the wrong way earlier when he refused to share why she hadn't heard from him while trying to pressure her to talk.

The rest of the road was smooth as she cruised through the rest of Illinois, Indiana, and then Michigan. She made it to her hometown around 4am and made her way straight to the house to drop Reese off and then to the hospital. As she was pulling into the hospital, Torine attempted to video chat Nikki, but she declined the call because her main priority was seeing Bibi.

As she walked into the hospital, she was required to sign-in, put on hand sanitizer and a face mask before walking to her room. After moving through each action swiftly, she rushed to Bibi's hospital room. As she approached the room, she saw her dad and sister straight ahead, and her uncles and cousins were in the family lounge area. Nikki could feel the heavy energy of the room before she even made it to the door.

She could tell at that moment that there wasn't any good news to prepare for. Before walking into the room, she was expecting the worst news possible. As she walked into the room, only her sister and dad were awake. They both jumped up and greeted with hugs and kisses on the cheek. They all immediately turned to look at Bibi and then back to each other. Nikki could see the fatigue and worry across their body and faces as both their eyes appeared to look sunken in from no sleep, worry, and crying.

"Any updates from the doctors?" Nikki asked them both. Both her sister and dad looked at each other at the same time, before her dad broke the silence.

"She is currently breathing with the help of the machine. They said her organs are failing and that she will die once we turn off the machine. I'm waiting until both brothers wake up before we give the doctors the final say," Her dad responded with a cracked voice.

"Are you telling me my Bibi isn't going to make it? Are you telling me I won't get a chance to hear my Bibi talk to me again?" Nikki asked frantically before the tears started pouring out like a water fountain.

Unable to hold the tears in, Nikki walked over to Bibi's bedside and grabbed her hand just like old times. As she rubbed her cold-wrinkled skin, she found herself craving the warmth she once had. That warm feeling, she used to get whenever she touched her Bibi was no longer there. Nikki could feel Bibi's soul slipping away from her body. She was no longer the same woman.

"Can you let me know the time you all plan to pull the plug? I want to be here" Nikki asked her dad.

He nodded and added, "of course."

"I'm going to go to the house and get some rest. I'll be back up here in the morning in the case I wake up before you all make the decision." Nikki responded.

The real reason Nikki wanted to go to the house, instead of staying at the hospital, was because she knew this would be the last night she would be able to spend in the presence of Bibi's home before everyone started visiting. Nikki lived with Bibi before graduating from high school and going off to college. She spent most of her time, growing up, with Bibi until she started working and building her own life. It was her senior year of high school when she moved in with Bibi full-time after her dad kicked her out.

Nikki stayed with her best friend Simone for a month before Bibi made her move in with her, instead. After she took Nikki in, her dad stopped talking to Bibi for a few months because he felt Nikki needed to learn some unknown lessons. Needless to say, they had a lot of issues between them that lived below the surface and Bibi was always there to be a safe space. All those years later, Nikki still had key access to Bibi's home. She wanted this last moment with her, alone.

As Nikki turned to tell her sister and dad bye, she walked over to her Bibi and kissed her on the forehead before saying to her softly, "I love you always and forever."

Nikki picked her head up and began walking to the door. Before making it to the door, her dad told her, "you don't have to leave if you don't want to. We can leave out if you want time with her alone."

"I'm ok. Her spirit is no longer in her body and I just want to go home," Nikki responded.

Both her sister and dad looked at her as if she was slightly off, but no one said anything. They simply looked at her and nodded to her goodnight as she gave both of them a hug one at a time.

Nikki left out the room and walked towards the elevator to return to the lobby that led to her car. She didn't even stop to say anything to anyone else, as she left. When she made it to the lobby, she started walking faster and faster towards the door leading to the parking lot. As she walked past the front desk, the staff person asked, "Is everything ok?" Nikki simply nodded and kept speed walking to the door.

When she made it to the car, she pressed the unlock button, opened the door, closed it and turned on the engine. As she shifted the car into drive, she found herself talking to herself. *This is really real life right now* she thought as she pulled out the parking lot.

Nikki made it to the house in about 5 minutes time. Of course, she was speeding, but luckily she wasn't pulled over by the police. In that moment, all she had on her mind was making it home to a familiar place.

When she pulled up to the front of the house, she noticed Bibi's car parked in the driveway stretched alongside the right side of the house. Nikki stopped the car and placed the gear into park, triggering the car doors to unlock when she turned off the ignition. Nikki quickly took off her seatbelt, opened the door, and hopped out the car slamming the door behind her. She went to the trunk of the car to take out her suitcase and computer bag to take in the house with her. As she walked up to the front door, she fiddled with her keys until she found the correct key to unlock the door.

As Nikki found the key and placed it in the door, she looked over to the right of the door and took notice of the mailbox she helped label when she was a child. That quick, she found herself in a nostalgic place with flashbacks of moments with Bibi. There were so many moments of her childhood that she cherished that made her feel good.

Nikki quickly shook off the trance she had found herself in, locked the door behind her, and proceeded to unlock the 2nd door. As she looked around the front porch before opening the second door, she realized that Bibi had collected more items and allowed them to pile up on the patio. She had a large stack of newspapers by the door, at the far end of the patio there were two lounge chairs with items piled on top of each other until it was hard to decipher what all was on the chairs. Along the wall was a china cabinet that extended about 6 feet long and 6 feet high. Stacked on top of the cabinet was a pile of books and Christmas items, with lights dangling along the sides.

This made Nikki think about a conversation she had with Bibi before, when they were discussing all the items in her house. Bibi was joking about how her sons were always complaining about how much stuff she had in the house.

"Everybody telling me I got too much stuff, well it's my stuff and y'all can worry about throwing it out when I die," Nikki heard Bibi saying in a memory which pushed her to let out a quick giggle.

Giggling to herself, Nikki walked through the second door and closed it behind her. She looked around the house and noticed everything looked the same as it had when she was last home. As she looked around, she thought about how connected she was to her home. *Home always finds a way back to your heart*, she thought to herself.

Nikki walked through the home and stopped at the dining room table. At the table was Bibi's bible turned to 2 Corinthians chapter 5. With all the highlights and her Sunday school book lying next to her bible, Nikki could tell she was studying and preparing for the next meeting.

She walked into the back bedroom, where she slept growing up. In the last year, Bibi had been sleeping in the back bedroom and the main bedroom in the front had become a full walk-in closet that still didn't seem to be enough space. The back bedroom was small, but livable. With a queen-sized bed, there was enough space for two dressers, a nightstand, and walking space. Although there were items stacked alongside the dressers, a person would be able to move things around to reach what they were looking for. Even the television from Nikki's childhood was still in the room with the same remote controller- 15 years later.

Nikki looked on top of the dresser, along the back wall, and noticed a picture from her childhood. In the picture was her, Bibi, her great grandmother, and great aunt. It looked like they were at their annual family reunion in the south, because of the scenery. They were posing in front of her Great Great Grandmother's grave at the family church.

This graveyard was a family graveyard, where everyone from the blood lineage was supposed to be buried at. Even if a family member lived in another state, it was strongly suggested for them to be flown to North Carolina and buried in the graveyard. Nikki remembered Bibi telling her that family tale, even though she didn't want to be buried there. She wanted to be buried with her husband in her current hometown. Nikki's Great Great Grandmother, Sophia, was born in 1888 in Gnorts, North Carolina to Jimmy and Binta Soldent who were both born a couple years before the abolishment of slavery. It was said that Grandma Sophia was named after her grandmother.

As a child, Nikki remembered learning that her Great Great Great Grandmother Binta was raised by her aunt after her mother was killed for behaving outside of how slaves were supposed to behave. That's all she remembered being told and she never asked any questions.

For some reason, there was something about this picture that made her want to take it home with her. Not only was Bibi in it, but her great grandmother and great aunt were in the picture as well. Nikki felt that would be the perfect item to have as a keepsake.

The last time Nikki visited home, Bibi gave her a quilt that was passed down to her from her mother, Nikki's great grandmother. Nikki hadn't slept with it yet but having it as a keepsake was all she needed to feel connected to the matriarchal lineage in her family. Since Bibi didn't have any daughters, she felt Nikki was the closest she would have to a daughter.

Nikki decided to take the picture, before anyone else did. She put it in the side pocket of her computer bag and went to the bathroom to get ready for bed. She was beyond tired by that time. While looking in the mirror, Nikki started thinking to herself, how much she loved Bibi and missed her.

Tired, Nikki walked into the living room to grab her suitcase and went back to the bathroom to finish getting ready for bed. As soon as Nikki finished in the bathroom, Reese came running up to her, jumping up and down for her attention. Nikki was so stuck in her head that she forgot Reese was there in the house, and him hiding away didn't help. She was sure the reason he was jumping on her was because he wanted to go outside.

"Ok, come on Reese, let's go outside," Nikki.

He ran so fast that he beat Nikki to the door. When Nikki made it to the door, she opened the first one and used the key by the door to open the 2nd one. Reese ran straight to the grass and lifted his leg to use the bathroom. Once he was done, he came running to the door to be let back into the house.

"Well, that was fast!" Nikki said to Reese with a joking tone, "Let's go to bed baby."

~4~

The Portal

Nikki was unable to get a restful sleep for the few hours she laid down before going back to the hospital. She found herself tossing and turning the entire time, partly because the sun had begun to rise as she was laying down to rest.

Even though she didn't get a lot of sleep, she was still able to get up and head to the hospital like she had slept for 10 hours straight. Nikki pulled up to the hospital before 11am, parked, and ran inside the building. When she got to the front desk, she signed in and ran to the elevators to get to Bibi's hospital room.

As she was coming off the elevator, she looked in the direction of the hospital room and something in her spirit didn't feel right. As she got closer, she noticed everyone crying and holding hands. In the room was her dad, sister, niece, nephew, both uncles, and two of her cousins. When Nikki walked in the room, she looked in the direction of Bibi, to see that the machines were no longer connected to her body. It's as if no one noticed Nikki walk into the room because they were all crying into their hands and each other's shoulders.

"Why aren't the machines on?" Nikki asked, startling them all.

"We had them turn the machines off a couple of hours ago," Nikki's uncle Edgar chimed in. "Hey Niece, I'm glad you were able to make it up here, especially with the emergency shut down," he continued while walking over to give Nikki a hug.

"Hey Uncle Edgar, of course I couldn't allow myself to not come see Bibi," Nikki responded.

Looking in the direction of her dad, Nikki asked, "What happened to you letting me know when you were going to do it?"

"We wanted to, but the brothers decided to do it earlier with just us," Her dad responded.

Nikki could feel the blood in her body beginning to boil over as her dad admitted that he didn't feel it was important for her to be there, especially after she had just drove 11 hours straight to be there. Instead of saying what she wanted to say, she chose to turn around and walk out the room.

As Nikki was walking out, she heard her uncle Remy say, "I guess she is mad now, she needs to understand the world doesn't revolve around her."

At first thought, Nikki wasn't going to respond to what was said, but something in her jolted and she decided to walk back into the room and give a piece of her mind.

"First off, yes, I am upset, especially since Bibi raised me like she was my mom, and I couldn't get the respect of at least being told that you decided to do it alone. This is nothing new with this family and then you had the nerve to talk about me as I walked away. So yes, I am upset because at 31 almost 32 years of life I still get treated like a child in a family full of judgement." Nikki shot back at her uncle.

"This has nothing to do with you and you are not Bibi's daughter, she was my mom. If you have a problem with how we decided to make decisions then that problem is with you and not us," Uncle Edgar chimed in.

Nikki looked at her dad to see if he would say anything, but he said nothing. He sat there looking at Bibi as if nothing was happening around him. He was in his own bubble, in somewhat of a trance. He had just lost his mom and now his daughter and brothers were arguing.

Nikki said to her Uncles, "Bibi was my mom and how dare you tell me that she wasn't. I have just the same amount of closeness to her as you."

"I really don't have time for your drama queen antics right now. Maybe you should leave and go to the house. We don't need that devil energy in here right now," Uncle Remy said.

"The devil?! Did you just call me the devil?!" Nikki asked her Uncle Remy furiously.

"I didn't say that, but if the shoe fits then maybe. You used to be so deep into church and then something happened, and you stopped. Maybe you'll find your way again one day," Uncle Remy responded back. "That's the only reason why you're acting like that right now," he continued.

"Did you really just say what the fuck I think you did? This is exactly why I worked to stay away from most of you all in this family, because of comments like this. I'm starting to think you have more devil in you than me!" Nikki shot.

"I think it's best for you to leave," Uncle Edgar jumped in.

"Dad, are you okay? Do you hear all of this?" Nikki asked while looking over at him.

"I just had to pull the plug on my mama. No, I'm not ok and I wish we didn't have to go through this right now." He responded.

Nikki, not knowing what to do or say, decided to turn around and leave the room.

"I refuse to be where I am not welcomed," Nikki said as she walked out of the room. "I wish you all well."

Looking in a daze, Nikki realized that she didn't want to be by her family. If she couldn't be with her Bibi, she didn't want to be around anyone else. Upset, Nikki made her way to her.

They really had me fucked up! This is why I don't like being around my family, they love to demonize people. Nikki thought to herself as she pressed on the brakes and the button to start the car.

That fast, Nikki made up her mind that she would not bring in her birthday with her family, so she called Torine.

Torine answered the call on the first ring.

"Hey Baby, how are you doing? I was worried about you." He answered.

"I'm ok. I don't think I want to be here with my family anymore. I'm actually thinking about grabbing my things and coming to see you. Can I stay with you a few days before I go back to Memphis?" Nikki asked.

"Of course, you can come here baby, what time do you think you will make it?" Torine asked.

"I'll keep you updated," she responded.

Nikki made her way back to the house to grab her things and Reese so they could make their way to the other side of the state. As Nikki finished putting all of her items in the car, her Uncles were pulling up to the house. She was trying to move fast and get in the car before they got out of the car, but she was too late.

"Nikki, we don't say these things because we don't like you, it's because when you stopped going to church you changed and the bible talks against that. I don't think mama would've wanted you near her body at the time of her crossing over," Uncle Remy said.

"Did you really just say that bullshit to my face? If I didn't love you and you weren't my uncle, I would give you a long list of choice words, instead I'm going to get in my car and leave because you're not worth the black on my ass," Nikki said before getting in her car and slamming the door. She was in such a hurry to get out of there she didn't even put on her seatbelt.

I don't care if I never see them again, Nikki thought angrily.

She picked up her phone and texted Torine to tell him that she was on her way. He immediately responded back with a location pin, "ok baby, see you soon, here is the address."

Nikki put the address in her GPS and started her journey. A two-and-a-half-hour journey to be exact. On her way to Torine's she stopped one time to get gas and then she finished the trip from there.

As she pulled into Torine's driveway, he came running out the door to greet her with a big smile. As soon as she turned the car off and stepped out, he gave her a big hug, which turned into him picking her up and her kicking her legs before he put her back down.

"Hey Baby! It feels so good to see you outside of a video call," He said grinning from cheek to cheek.

"I know right! I wish it was under better circumstances, but that's not how life decided to work out," Nikki responded back.

Next thing she knew, Torine picked her up again, looked into her eyes, and started kissing her passionately while placing her on the hood of her car. They kissed for a couple of minutes before they decided to come up for air. They both were breathing heavily as if the kiss had taken their breath and energy away.

Right when they stopped kissing, Nikki's phone rang in the car. She knew it had to be one of her family members, because the person called again after she ignored the first one. Both Nikki and Torine looked at each other and then in the direction of the car where the ringing was coming from.

"Do you want to answer it?" Torine asked while still holding Nikki. Her legs were wrapped tightly around him, and she didn't want to be put down.

"The reality is, I don't know if I want to or not. I feel like they are just going to piss me off more," Nikki answered him.

"Do you want to go in the house instead?" Torine asked.

"Yes, I'd actually like to take a shower and relax," she responded with a softened voice.

They both looked each other in the eyes and kissed once more. "I want you to get in the shower with me," Nikki expressed.

He looked deep into her eyes, grinned, and replied, "Yea, ok."

"Well put me down, so I can race you there," Nikki said with a giggle trying to push away.

"What if I wanted to carry you?" Torine asked.

"Just make sure you come back out and get my bags," Nikki said with a grin on her face, before biting her bottom lip.

As Nikki finished her statement, Torine started walking her to the porch connected to the back door. As he waddled up each step, Nikki felt his manhood beginning to bulge through his pants. As she felt him beginning to throb, her vagina started getting wet and she envisioned riding him for the first time. As much as she wanted to tell him that she felt and wanted him, she decided to remain quiet and enjoy him carrying her instead. It made her feel like a dainty princess in one of those fairy tales she heard growing up.

Torine carried Nikki into the living room and laid her on the couch alongside the right side of the room. He quickly turned away and made his way back outside to get Nikki's bags from the car. Nikki looked around the house and couldn't believe she was there, after seeing it every day for the last 2 months via video calls. Along the main wall, he had a plaque of Kwame Beans, a famous baseball player that died in January. He was Torine's favorite player and his death definitely affected him.

Life can be so short, Nikki thought to herself as she thought about Kwame and Bibi.

Torine appeared shortly after, carrying Nikki's suitcase, purse, and Reese's bed. Reese was following behind him wagging his tail excitedly.

"You want me to leave your suitcase down here or take it up stairs?" Torine asked.

"You can leave it right here, for right now. I can get my shower items and lounge clothes together," she responded.

"Let me go turn on the shower," Torine said, as he headed to the bathroom to prepare the shower.

As Nikki listened to Torine fiddle with the shower, she opened her suitcase and started taking out items she needed to shower with and clothes to put on after.

"What color towel do you want, baby?" Torine yelled, as he opened the bathroom closet door.

"I'm not picky babe, it doesn't matter, but thank you for asking," she answered. For some reason, him asking her that made her lady parts tingle. Nikki hadn't been with anyone in months, but she knew she wanted to give it to Torine. It was something about him that made her comfortable, she wanted to be with him as long as life allowed.

Nikki closed her suitcase and zipped it up before standing and heading to the bathroom. As she walked in the bathroom, Torine was walking out of the bathroom, while explaining where everything was located for Nikki to use. As he continued walking out of the bathroom, Nikki asked, "where are you going?"

"I'm going to be out here waiting for you," Torine responded.

"I really wanted you to take a shower with me," she said in a child-like voice.

Torine looked down toward Nikki, as he stood at least a foot taller than her. "You sure you want to?" He responded.

"Yes, I need some help washing my back," Nikki answered with a smile as she started undressing in front of him.

She started with her shirt and then began unzipping her pants and pulling them down slowly.

"Are you going to help me wash my back?" Nikki asked.

"I got you baby," Torine responded while lifting his arms to take his shirt off.

They both stared at each other as they stripped off their clothes. With every motion, Torine walked closer and closer to Nikki, until they were chest to chest. Once he felt the warmth of her breasts against his chest, he put both his hands behind Nikki's head and leaned down to kiss her. As they kissed, Nikki felt her knees shake and the juices from her honey pot started running down her leg. She pulled away immediately, when she realized what happened.

"Let's get in the water baby," she demanded, while turning to open the shower curtain. She stepped in with one foot at a time, before turning for him to get in after.

Nikki leaned across Torine, grabbed the washcloth, and wet it under the running water. When the washcloth became soaked, Nikki reached her arms over his chest and squeezed the cloth until all the water was drained out and running down his body. She looked up into his eyes and pulled his head down and initiated the most passionate kiss ever. Torine ran his hands down Nikki's body with an emphasis on every curve, until he made it to the bottom of her buttcheeks. He cuffed both cheeks with each hand, which made Nikki jump. He quickly turned her around and slightly arched her back, so now her chest was against the back of the shower while he was behind her pulsating.

By this time, Nikki was breathing heavily from the excitement and connection. She imagined feeling him inside of her honey pot, taking up all the space, as she looked back and saw his manhood standing at attention. Torine took his arms and wrapped them around Nikki until he was grasping her breasts with one hand, choking her gently with the other, and kissing on her neck simultaneously. With one hand playing with her nipple, he took his other from her neck and began to move south toward her vagina. *Nikki's body quivered from his touch.*

Once he made it, he started fingering Nikki's vagina by first slowly playing with the clitoris with his pointer finger, until his middle finger was eventually pushing in and out of her vaginal hole.

Nikki moaned in enjoyment as he continued kissing, touching, and playing with her at the same time. Torine sped up and added another finger to help him push her g-spot. As soon as Nikki felt herself beginning to cum, he stopped, turned her around and got on his knees.

Torine was showing his true zodiac sign, because he ate her vagina while the shower water was running over his head until Nikki orgasmed multiple times. There was no body washing taking place in the shower, just orgasm after orgasm, until Nikki made Torine stop. Her legs were so weak, that she was unable to continue standing up in the shower, so she slid down and sat on her butt, while the water hit both of them.

Soaking wet, Torine got out of the shower and picked Nikki up. He carried her into his room and laid her across the bed still soaking wet.

"Come here Zaddy, I want to feel you inside of me," Nikki said, as he climbed on top of the bed and over her.

He took his hand and started playing with her vagina, which was making her more wet. With his finger still inside of her, he slowly inserted his penis. While pressing her g-spot, he continued to slide in and out as they both moaned in ecstasy. He moved his other hand and wrapped it around Nikki's neck, giving it a squeeze. In an instant, Nikki saw a bright green light flash before her eyes, before closing them. She didn't think to ask if he saw it too, everything was feeling too good.

Nikki and Torine made love for the rest of the day and all night. The only times they stopped were to take Reese outside, eat, and use the bathroom. They basically feasted on each other the entire night.

The next morning, Nikki woke up feeling slightly wheezy and her vagina was quite sore. She immediately thought to herself how he wore her, and apparently her vagina out. She rolled over and saw he was still sleeping, so she kissed him on the forehead, rolled back over and got out the bed to use the bathroom.

As Nikki sat on the toilet, she started having flashbacks of their sexual escapade the night before. She broke all of her rules with Torine. Not only did they have sex unprotected, but she also let him cum inside of her. When Nikki made it back to the room, Torine was still asleep in the bed. Instead of waking him up, she decided to make breakfast and work on homework for about an hour until he woke up from his slumber.

When Torine woke up, he came walking into the living room with his arms stretched wide and mouth wide-open.

"I guess that means I put it on you last night, huh?" Nikki asked jokingly.

"Baby, I don't know what all happened last night, but I can tell you that it was fucking magical with the fucking pun intended. We were made for each other," Torine responded with a big smile on his face before kissing Nikki on the forehead.

"Did you make me some breakfast too? I thought I was supposed to be feeding you," He added.

"Of course, I made enough for you too, you gonna come in the kitchen with me to make the plate?" Nikki flirted.

"Lead the way my Queen," he responded.

While they were in the kitchen, Nikki's phone started ringing. When it stopped ringing, it started back again. She knew at that moment, that it was someone from her family calling.

"Babe, maybe you should answer it, in the case something is wrong," Torine suggested, while opening the fridge door.

"You're right," Nikki agreed while walking to grab her phone from the couch. She picked it up and saw it was her cousin Jamille calling. She wasn't at the hospital when everything happened, so maybe she was just calling to see if Nikki was coming home.

"Hey love!" Nikki answered the phone.

"Hey Cuz! How are you doing?" Jamille asked.

"I'm doing ok, just relaxing with my boyfriend," Nikki answered while taking a seat on the couch.

"Awe, I bet it feels good having someone there with you," Jamille responded.

"Yea, it really does, because yea…" Nikki said with hesitation in her voice. She didn't want to open the gates to discuss what happened at the hospital, but something in her told her it was coming.

"I know, it's a hard time for all of us. I know your birthday is tomorrow, do you have anything planned?" Jamille asked.

"No, I just want to relax and keep my mind clear as possible." Nikki answered.

"I totally understand," Jamille hesitantly responded before going silent for a few seconds. "I'm sure someone has probably told you already," Jamille continued.

"Told me what?" Nikki asked.

"Were you planning on coming to the funeral?" Jamille asked.

"No, I don't even know when it is," Nikki shot back.

"Good, because we don't need that devil energy here anyways," Nikki heard her aunt Tangie say in the background quietly.

"Did you call me on speaker phone? I wasn't talking that loud for her to hear me. I promise this family ain't shit." Nikki said to Jamille before hanging up on her.

"I swear they get on my nerves with all that fake shit, it's like I see right through them." Nikki said to Torine angrily.

"You don't think that you may have overreacted a little bit? Torine asked.

"Overreacted? Did you really just ask me that? You don't call someone on 3-way if you're not trying to start drama," Nikki shot back.

"Nevermind, let's just act like it didn't happen," he responded.

"Do you have any weed I can smoke?" Nikki asked. I didn't bring any up with me.

"I have one rolled up for you upstairs, I'll go get it," Torine responded as he walked fast-paced towards the stairs to get the hemp roll.

Nikki couldn't believe what just happened. She didn't know when the funeral was planned for, and she didn't know if she was going to go back to visit before heading back to Memphis. That phone call was an indicator that she didn't need to go back. She realized that she had to make her peace with Bibi's death without a funeral.

Torine came running down the stairs.

"Here you go baby," he said while passing her the hemp roll.

"Thank you," Nikki responded while grabbing it and the lighter he had in his other hand.

For the next few hours, they sat on the bed cuddled while watching television. Torine tried to have sex multiple times, but Nikki kept refusing. He thought she was refusing because of what happened earlier, but she was refusing because she had a lot on her mind. Silence was the smartest option, in her head.

Randomly, while lying there, Nikki concluded that she wanted to bring in her birthday alone. It was her 32nd birthday and that was considered a milestone year because 32 was always her favorite number. She looked over at the clock next to the television, and saw it was almost 3pm.

If she left within the next hour, she could make it home by midnight to bring in her birthday. The hardest part was figuring out how she would tell Torine that she was going to go home instead of staying there with him. As much as she wanted to stay with him, she had a strong urge to be alone for her birthday.

While lying on the bed, Nikki turned to face Torine. As their eyes locked, she started talking.

"I Love you baby and I really enjoyed this time we had together. I think I want to bring in my birthday at home, so I'm going to head back to Memphis," She said, while lowering her head.

"What? Tonight? I wanted to do something special for us," Torine said in a surprised tone.

"Yea, like, in the next 30 minutes. I really just want to be by myself and think. A lot has been happening and I want to be alone for my birthday," she responded.

"You cannot be serious right now!" He shot back in a disgusted tone.

"You're supposed to be coming to visit me in a few weeks anyways babe, so it won't be that long until we see each other again," Nikki responded. "Truth be told, if my trip wasn't cancelled, I'd be lying on a beach alone, right now anyways," she added with a giggle.

Torine wasn't laughing, but he could tell it was a losing situation for him if he decided to try and convince Nikki to change her mind. This was especially true, as he watched her start to get out of the bed and begin scrambling to organize her things.

It took Nikki 20 minutes to get all her items and Reese packed into the car. As she sat in the driver's seat, Torine stood at the door of the car and they stared at each other for what seemed like almost a minute before she brought his head closer to hers for a kiss.

"I love you baby," Nikki told Torine.

"I love you too, please be safe!" Torine pleaded with Nikki.

"I will be baby, I'm about to share my location with you, so you will be able to track my progress home. Is that cool?" Nikki asked.

"Yes ma'am, I want to talk to you too though," He said with a laugh at the end.

"I'll keep you updated baby," Nikki said, as she lowered herself to get into the car.

After buckling herself in, she pressed her foot on the brake and turned the engine on. When the car turned on, Torine closed the door for Nikki and she rolled the window down. Torine leaned into the car window and gave her one last kiss goodbye, then looked in the back and told Reese, "Take care of your mama for me," and laughed before hitting the roof of the car.

"Love you baby and happy early birthday," Torine said as he began to walk backwards from the car.

Nikki blew him a kiss and reversed her car out the driveway. He stood there watching her until her car was no longer visible. Nikki plugged up her phone, turned on her music, and set her gps for the travel home.

The road was clear for Nikki as she traveled back to Memphis. Shortly after stopping for gas the second time, Nikki noticed she was going to be bringing her birthday in on the highway with Reese. She was 3 hours away from home, but her birthday was 2 hours away. Nikki put on her new playlist and set her cruise control.

By the time the playlist ended, it was 5 minutes before midnight. *Here I am, getting ready to turn 32*, Nikki thought to herself as she took a glance at the time and then rearview mirror.

As her eyes returned to the road, she noticed a bright flash of light in the sky ahead of her. It was hard to decipher what the light was, which made Nikki watch the skies much closer. Not 1 minute later, the bright flash happened again, but this time Nikki was able to make out what it resembled. It looked like some kind of portal from the action movies you only see on television. It was colored green, red, blue, and purple which reminded Nikki of a dream she had earlier that year. It was spinning so fast; it was hard to see in what direction. As Nikki found herself staring at the portal, a creature came flying out of the hole and landed on top of the car.

At that point, Nikki started getting nervous and afraid of what was going to happen, which forced her to panic. She slammed on the breaks to see if the creature would reveal itself; almost jerking herself into whiplash. Unfortunately, the creature still could not be seen. As she started speeding up, she watched the roof of her car to see if there was movement.

Am I seeing things right now? Nikki asked herself while she blinked her eyes profusely. "What the hell is going on?" She screamed out loud while watching the road and the portal opening in the sky ahead of her.

At that moment, she looked at the dashboard and realized her birthday was in less than a minute. Her heart started racing because she wanted to be excited, but she was growing increasingly more nervous, as the creature was still missing and there was an open portal in front of her. As soon as the clock struck midnight, Nikki felt her car lifting off the road. She hadn't done anything different and her cruise control was still set. She was no longer moving forward; she was moving upward.

"What the hell is going on?!" Nikki yelled nervously. As she looked around her, she saw the road become further and further away. The lights from other cars were at a far distance and she was quickly approaching the opening to the portal.

Next thing Nikki knew, her car was flying into the portal. As the car shot through the portal, she was no longer driving during the night, but was sitting in a drop-top sports car, parked on the beachside with Reese. Nikki looked around, searching for other people. Unfortunately, the only other living thing she saw were birds walking along the beachside.

As soon as Nikki started opening her car door, she noticed a figure walking towards her from the water. Nikki squinted her eyes attempting to make out who this figure was, walking towards her. Oddly, as the person got closer, Nikki found herself feeling more comfortable with the situation. Something in her felt peaceful, as if her nervousness faded the closer the person got. When they got within 5 feet of Nikki's car, she spoke out and said, "Welcome my Nia." Nikki immediately noticed the voice from one of her past dreams.

"Who are you? Who is Nia?" Nikki began asking the person. By this time, she had the chance to see a little more of her. Even though she was cloaked from head to toe, Nikki could notice she had dark skin, fiery red eyes, and she was about 5'5."

Her voice sounded like the perfect harmony, a mixture between soprano, alto, and tenor in one.

"I am of you and you are Nia," she responded.

"My name is Nikki and what do you mean you are me? Where are we at?" Nikki asked rapidly while looking around her.

"My dear, you know me, but you are not ready to be revealed to all of me and what I have to offer," she said before pausing and finishing her response. "Nikki is your shucra name. Your birth name is Nia."

Confused, Nikki asked, "What is a shucra name? How do you know me?"

"You are a smart woman Nia; you are a chosen one and it will all make sense to you really soon," she responded. "As long as you keep asking questions, you will soon understand."

"Where am I making it to? Where am I supposed to be going?" Nikki asked.

"It's not where you're supposed to be going, it's where you've already been. Just make sure you watch your surroundings and who you trust. You're 32 now, which makes you a target." She answered.

"What do you mean? Why are you talking in circles? What does 32 mean?" Nikki asked.

Turning to walk away, she responded, "Life is cyclical just like a circle. I talk from what I am, because what I am speaks for all. Most importantly, you will see soon enough. I know you are getting tired from all that driving, I hope you get a good night's sleep my dear."

Looking dumbfounded, Nikki asked, "when will I see you again?"

She responded, "When you need me most. But I'm always there. Happy return Nia, I'll see you later," right before vanishing.

"Ok, so how am I supposed to get home now?" Nikki asked out loud.

Nikki looked around and a voice told her to get in the car and start driving. So, that's what she did. Once she got her seatbelt attached, reversed out of her parking spot and started driving, she suddenly entered the portal once more, but this time her car was parked outside of her home. She was home and didn't have to finish the rest of her drive. Confused by everything that had happened, she looked up at the sky and thanked the mysterious woman she had just encountered.

"Happy fucking Birthday to Me," Nikki said as she unbuckled her seatbelt and got out the car.

~5~

The Visit

A few weeks had passed since that magical moment Nikki experienced the night of her birthday. She couldn't stop thinking about it. Every time she thought about telling someone about what she experienced she either got awkwardly quiet or an internal voice told her that it wasn't a good time. No one would understand what it was that she experienced, even Torine started acting differently.

Ever since her birthday, their communication had become more controlled. They still talked daily, but they only video chatted with each other every other day. They also cut down on the amount of time they stayed on the phone with each other, each time. The country opened the airports a week ago, so Torine was able to buy a plane ticket versus having to drive to visit Nikki.

Even though it felt like they were going through a rough patch in their relationship, she was still excited to pick him up from the airport. They had a lot planned for his weekend there. They were going bowling after she picked him up, the next day they were going to the Civil Rights Museum and Beale Street to end the night, before his plane left on Sunday morning.

It was 4:30 pm when Nikki received a text message from Torine that read, "We are landing now." After that message, she started getting ready to leave the house. Before leaving, she looked around the house to make sure everything was clean, and nothing was out of place. *I don't know why I'm acting like I care*, Nikki thought to herself.

She slid on her flip flops by the kitchen entrance, grabbed her purse, and opened the door. While closing the door with one hand, she used the other hand to fiddle with her keys until she found the key needed to lock the front door. After locking the main and screen door, she used the car key-fob to unlock the door. Once she was settled into the car, she put her foot on the gas pedal and started the engine.

As she drove through the parking lot to the main street, she started getting butterflies. She was excited and nervous to see Torine again, and to have him visit her. As much as she knew they would enjoy each other, she couldn't deny the changing energy that had been happening between the two. To keep from thinking about what could happen, she started thinking about the good things that could happen.

Nikki pulled up to the airport a little before 5pm and it just so happened that Torine was calling her at the same time.

"We must be divinely connected, because I just pulled into the airport. Are you down at baggage claim yet?" Nikki asked with a smile on her face.

"Yes! I told you- you are forever mine baby!" He responded. "I'm outside door number 3 waiting for you... oh wait, I think I see you," he finished as he walked towards the curb.

They both hung up as Nikki pulled her car along the curb, next to Torine and ended the call. As she was stopping the car, she was unbuckling her seatbelt simultaneously to make the process of getting out of the car faster.

Nikki didn't wait for Torine to come open the door for her, before she decided to swing it open herself and hop out of the car. Leaving the door open, Nikki ran to the passenger side of the car and jumped into Torine's arms. Torine was thrown off balance which made him scramble to get his balance back proper.

"I am so excited that you are here baby! This weekend is going to be such a good time, I can feel it!" Nikki said to Torine. Even though she had a slight nervousness about the visit, she still was hopeful for a great time together.

"I know! What's first on the agenda?" Torine asked while walking to the driver's door to close.

"First, we are going to drop your items off at the house then head straight to the bowling alley to enjoy some bowling and bar food!" Nikki said excitedly.

"Awe shoot, you sure you're ready to get your ass beat? I don't want you being mad at me during the whole trip!" Torine asked sarcastically.

"Boy boo!" Nikki shot back. "Don't forget you're giving me a 100-pin handicap, so I better win," Nikki added while laughing.

Torine walked to the back of the car and attempted to open the trunk. "Do you want me to put this in the trunk or back seat?" He asked.

"You can just put it back here, since we are going to the house first," Nikki responded, while opening the back passenger door.

Torine dragged his suitcase to the back door and tossed it on the seat. Nikki stood back quickly, to keep from being hit by the swinging suitcase. "Dang bae, you gonna knock me out," she said sarcastically while laughing.

She started walking around to the driver's side of the car. As she was walking back to the driver's seat, Torine ran around the front of the car to reach the door first.

"I don't want you touching your car door whenever I'm around. Deal?" Torine asked while opening the driver's door for Nikki to get in the car.

"Deal" She responded as she ducked down to get into the car while looking up at Torine with a grin on her face. Torine waited for her to tuck her legs in before closing the door behind her.

Nikki fastened her seatbelt and turned the engine over, as Torine walked to the passenger side of the car, and got in. As he got in, he noticed the seat was close to the dashboard, forcing him to adjust the seat for his long legs. Nikki looked over and saw him pushing the seat back and started to laugh.

"What are you laughing at?" Torine asked.

"Your tall ass in my car, that's what," she responded while still laughing.

After checking her mirrors, Nikki pulled out into the traffic lane and drove towards the airport exit. Torine seemed to enjoy the sites of the trip back

The Visit

to the house as his eyes followed each moving object encouraging him to ask questions regarding everything that intrigued him.

It didn't take long for them to make it to the house from the airport. When Nikki finished parking the car, Torine opened the door before she even turned the car off. "You bet not touch that door," he said as he was getting out of the car.

Torine made his way to Nikki's door and opened it for her. Once she put one leg out of the car, he moved to the back door and opened it to retrieve his suitcase. Nikki got out of the car and closed the door behind her. As she walked to the house door to unlock it, Torine was behind her looking around the area.

"How are your neighbors here?" He asked with a slight bit of concern in his voice.

"They are pretty good, it feels like we are a little community who looks out for each other," She responded. While talking, she turned her head to look at Torine sideways. "I told you I lived in the hood. For some reason, I feel safer here than in places with a bunch of people who don't look like me," Nikki shrugged.

"I didn't mean anything by it. I was just wondering. It's my job to make sure my baby is safe and ok at all times," Torine justified while walking up to kiss Nikki on the neck while she was opening the door.

Looking at him with a side eye, "Yea okay." Nikki walked through the door first and Torine followed behind her with his luggage. He placed them on the floor near the entrance and then closed the door behind himself.

"What time do you want to hit up the bowling alley?" Torine asked.

"I'm ready to go now, if you are?" she responded.

"I mean, it was a long flight, and I would love to have a kiss from my woman." Torine said while pulling Nikki towards him. Nikki willingly turned around and looked at Torine with bedroom eyes while asking, "What kind of kiss are you talking about exactly?" She started biting her bottom lip from just thinking about him kissing both sets.

"How about you sit down and find out." Torine said while pulling her slowly towards the couch. "And nah, I don't mean for you to sit on yo ass," he added.

"Where do you want me to sit then, Zaddy?" Nikki asked playfully.

Torine answered quickly, "On my face," before licking his lips.

"Say less." Nikki started pulling down her panties. "I want you to lay on the floor," she demanded.

With no questions asked, Torine laid on the floor, in the exact spot she directed him to lay. With her dress still on, Nikki stood over Torine and commanded, "Say please."

Torine looked up and all he saw was the sweet fruit he couldn't wait to taste. As he licked his lips, he noticed Nikki was so wet that it was starting to run down her leg.

"Can I please have what's mine?" Torine asked.

"Keep on and you'll be leaving here a married man," Nikki responded while giggling.

"How about a married man and I put a baby in you?" Torine responded while pulling Nikki down to his face.

Torine had given Nikki oral for about 20 minutes by the time she orgasmed 5 times and couldn't feel her legs anymore. He didn't want sex, that was never his plan. He wanted to satisfy his woman and relax for a moment in her presence. They laid there on the floor looking at each other and talking, until they both fell asleep.

It was around 7:30 pm when they woke up from their quick joint nap. Not wanting to miss a moment of the weekend together, they got up and went to the bowling alley. Of the 5 games they played, Torine won 4 of them. Of course, Nikki accused him of cheating, by weakening his opponent before battle.

When they got back to the house, it was almost midnight and they were still full of energy. Instead of going straight to bed, they decided to watch a movie on the internet. They weren't 15 minutes into the movie before Torine had Nikki bent over on the couch. After about 20 minutes on the couch, they moved to the bedroom. When Nikki entered the room, she turned on the lights surrounding her bed and let loose the canopy net to entrap them.

"This is some sexy shit," Torine said, while looking around. "This is the perfect vibe."

Nikki scooted back to the head of the bed, while Torine stood at the foot of the bed watching her. Using her right index finger, she motioned for him to come towards her. He immediately started crawling towards her on the bed and they made love under the canopy lights, until the bed sheets were completely dampened by their juices and sweat all night. The sun had started to rise when they both started falling asleep in each other's arms.

"I'm happy we met each other baby, I feel like you understand me. We read together, we talk, we communicate, you're everything I have ever wanted in a man," Nikki said to Torine, while playing with his beard.

"It feels good to have a woman that I can be myself with. Thank you for making me feel heard. That's why you're my future wife," Torine responded while planting a gentle kiss on Nikki's forehead.

"Wife?" Nikki asked out of surprise.

"I'm serious if you are!" Torine quickly responded. "The way I'm feeling, we can elope tomorrow," He finished while planting a gentle kiss on Nikki's lips.

Nikki closed her eyes and started breathing faster and louder before responding, "We were made for each other." She smiled and looked up at him before continuing, "Tomorrow, we are going to the Civil Rights museum, I'm taking you to a Barbecue spot downtown to experience some real soul food and music."

"Oh, you have an eventful day planned out I see. This is going to be a good time, and I get to get some of that good Southern Moonshine!" Torine added in excitedly.

They talked for another 10 minutes before going to sleep in each other's arms. When Nikki woke up the next day, it was around 12 noon. While Torine was still asleep, she started preparing brunch for them both, before getting the day started. The museum was slated to close at 7pm, so it was imperative that they arrived for the tour by 4pm. Torine was still sleeping like a baby and Nikki didn't want to interrupt his sleep.

I wonder if he was serious about the marriage. Nikki started thinking and asking herself as she made them brunch. She immediately brushed off the conversation, turned on music and finished cooking. For some reason, that wasn't something she wanted to think about, especially since she was still floating on cloud 9 from the night before. When she finished cooking, she woke Torine up from his slumber to come eat.

By the time they finished eating and getting dressed it was around 3:30pm, which gave them ample time to make their way to the museum and explore all the artifacts and historical facts related to civil rights and the history of black people in the United States.

The tour of the museum took them about 2-hours to complete without a tour guide. This was perfect because it left them time to visit the Blues Hall on Beale street to eat and enjoy their happy hour vibes. By the time they finished the tour, their arms were locked, and their energy was heavy in response to the various exhibits they visited.

"How did you feel about the museum?" Nikki asked Torine as he opened the door for her to exit the building.

"It was powerful and heavy!" He responded with extra bass in an attempt to keep from cracking. "It was emotional reading about the history of the slave trade, the spiritual background of black folks, and just how we have been treated over time," He added. My family lineage got lucky. My Great Great Great Great Grandfather was gifted a plantation after slavery ended because the owner was planning to move oversees."

"Whatttt?! Talk about luck of the draw to build generational wealth," Nikki responded back with a laugh. "So that's why your family looks so well off?" She asked.

"Whatever you want to call it." He added in with a nervous laugh. "I try not to dive too deep into it and just live my life. You feel me?" He asked rhetorically.

"Alright, enough heavy stuff for the day, Beale street is like a mile from here so it's best that we drive to get closer to the restaurant. When we are done eating and enjoying happy hour, we can visit some other places that are within walking distance." Nikki stated.

"I'm with whatever you're with baby," Torine responded as he reached to open the car door for Nikki. He waited until she was in the car before closing the door and walking to the passenger side to get in the car.

It took them less than 5 minutes to arrive at the barbecue spot where they were going to take part in enjoying some good music and food. When they arrived, they chose to sit at the bar so they could take advantage of the happy hour specials. Nikki was always planning to be the designated driver while Torine enjoyed himself with spirits and some Memphis barbecue.

Torine was 6 drinks in by the time the band came out to start playing their latest hits and covers of throwback hit songs. The first song they played was *Distant Lover,* by Marvin Gaye, who just so happened to be Torine's favorite artist of all time. As soon as the song started playing, he started swaying from side to side. Torine was just finishing his 6th drink but his swaying had a strong resemblance to a drunk uncle looking to find the beat to dance with.

"Ahhhh, this is my sonnnnng! Come slow dance with me baby," Torine said while standing up and grabbing Nikki's hand to stand with him.

Nikki jumped up before Torine could finish his sentence. Why would she turn down the opportunity to experience two things that she loved at the same time? As they slowly danced to the band and synchronized melodies of singing between the main singer and back-up, it felt as if Marvin wrote the chorus especially for them.

Heeeeeaven knoowsss thhhhat I lonnnng for yooooou, Torine started singing in Nikki's ear. He was slightly slurring the words, but Nikki knew what he meant. She closed her eyes and stood on her toes to give him a soft sensual kiss on the lips and said, "You have me baby."

She slowly opened her eyes and rested her head on his chest. As she laid her head down, she looked over towards the other end of the bar. There was a man and a woman talking, who looked really familiar to Nikki. She didn't realize who they were until they turned around. She had seen the woman before in one of her dreams, but not the man.

Feeling as if she saw a ghost, Nikki quickly closed her eyes tight hoping she was hallucinating. To her surprise, when she opened them back, they were still there- but this time they were both staring at her.

"I need to go to the bathroom," Nikki said to Torine before running off to the. Torine appeared confused as to why Nikki ran off so fast. He looked dumbfounded for a moment before heading to the bar counter to order another drink.

"Let me get a double moonshine and a rum and coke," Torine said, before turning back to enjoy the music.

Meanwhile, Nikki was in the bathroom throwing water on her face, trying to figure out what and who she had seen. She noticed the woman from the night of her birthday, when she experienced the vortex. It was the same woman she talked to, who called her Nia. The man on the other hand, she hadn't seen him before, but it made her question who he was even more.

What the hell is going on? Nikki thought to herself.

"You're waking up my love," Someone spoke behind her, forcing her to jump from surprise. She noticed the voice. It was the woman from her dream and birthday.

Nikki quickly turned around to be greeted by the mysterious woman she had met almost a month prior. This time, she was closer and able to see just how beautiful the woman was. She had a deep chocolate skin tone, with eyes that looked like they were made of glass with blue colored Irises, although last time they were red. Her skin was smooth, and she had a mole on the left side of her face, slightly above her eyebrow, the same place as Nikki.

"Who are you? Am I dreaming right now?" Nikki asked nervously. At that point, she was beginning to question the difference between her dreams and reality.

"This is far from a dream, my love. My name is Sookani, I'm your guide," She answered.

"My guide, what do you mean?" Nikki asked Sookani. She was getting confused as to what was happening and why she was experiencing everything.

"We were meant to meet, and you are destined to complete so much on this earth," Sookani responded.

"What am I supposed to accomplish? Why did you call me Nia? Who was that man out there?" Nikki rapidly asked, before Sookani put her finger up to her lips- motioning for Nikki to fall silent.

"Just be careful and pass the tests placed in front of you. That's all you must focus on at this time," Sookani said in an attempt to reassure Nikki.

She handed Nikki an envelope and instructed her to not tell anyone about it and to not open it until exactly 24 hours from that time. Nikki looked down at her phone to see that it was 8:30pm. When she looked up, Sookani was gone, and Nikki was now in the bathroom alone. She walked by each bathroom stall, pushing the doors in to make sure no one else was in the bathroom. After finding all the stalls were empty, Nikki left the bathroom to see Torine flailing around the dance floor with another drink in his hand.

"Heeeeeey Baby, I missed you! Come give me a kiss!" Torine yelled to Nikki from across the room.

Nikki rolled her eyes behind her head and walked slowly towards Torine. *Should I tell him about what just happened in the bathroom?* Nikki asked herself.

She quickly remembered that Sookani told her to not tell anyone. Plus, she had a good feeling that Torine wouldn't understand her anyway, especially after her birthday.

It was that moment that she made the decision to not tell Torine about the experience she just had in the bathroom. Instead, she walked up behind him as he was dancing with his eyes closed. He turned around and gave her a big sloppy kiss on the forehead. "Hey baby, I'm having so much fun. I just took a few more shots of that moonshine and now I'm feelinnnng goooooodddd," he said while starting to slur his words again.

Nikki decided that she should start monitoring Torine's drinks. He had drinks before she went to the bathroom and he said he had a few shots of moonshine while she was gone. Moonshine was illegal where he was from, for a reason, and he was definitely drunk at that point.

Nikki walked over to the bar to get a glass of water for Torine, to help him start sobering up. As the bartender walked over to Nikki, she noticed his face was blue. All of his features were human, but his face was the color blue. Confused, Nikki asked him for a glass of water. When he walked away to get the water, Nikki tapped the man's shoulder next to her and asked, "what color is his skin?"

The stranger responded back, confused, "is that a trick question?"

Confused as to why the person would think that, she reassured him that it wasn't a trick question.

"He's black," the man responded before walking away from Nikki, and looking back shaking his head.

Great, now he thinks I'm some crazy drunk girl asking people random questions, Nikki thought to herself.

"Thank you, sir," Nikki said to the bartender before asking him, "is your skin blue?"

The bartender looked at Nikki, with raised eyebrows and a snarky grin, before responding, "Well damn, I grew up being told I was so black that I was blue, but this is the first time I have heard it at work."

"I am so sorry; I think these drinks are kicking in!" Nikki lied, while leaving a dollar tip on the counter and walking away. *Am I really that damn stupid?* Nikki asked herself while walking back towards Torine on the dance floor. After passing him the water to drink, Nikki took a sip of the drink he had in his hand in exchange.

"How about we make our way home after you finish this drink?" Nikki asked Torine.

"I like how that sounds sexaaaay mamaaaa!" Torine said while humping the air.

It took about 15 minutes for Torine to finish the drinks and pay their bill for the night. When they left out the bar, the strip was lined with people walking, talking, and drinking amongst each other. When they made it to the car, Torine went straight to the passenger side of the car and waited for Nikki to unlock the door.

"Oh, you got some drinks in your system and you can't open my door now?" Nikki said jokingly while pressing the unlock button on the car and opening her car door to get in.

Running to the driver side of the car, Torine responded, "oh baby, you know I didn't mean anything by that," before closing the door behind her and running back to the passenger side of the car and getting in.

Torine started hitting himself upside the head repeatedly and saying, "stop doing dumb shit bro, do what you're supposed to."

"Are you okay baby?" Nikki interrupted.

"Yes, baby I'm ok. Sorry I forgot to open your door. You shouldn't have to see me like this."

"I understand, you're just feeling good," Nikki responded.

"This whole day has been interesting, and it all started at the damn museum. Don't you know I saw the name of the plantation my family inherited? Jim Ramsey, one of the harshest plantation owners in all of North Carolina... yup, that's him! That's why I had us take a picture," Torine said.

"I grew up playing with his bloodline. Hell, that's how I learned how to bowl so well: Jake Ramsey. I was best friends with his son until we moved to Michigan when I was in high school. Dad sold his stake in the plantation and decided to invest in the automotive industry up north."

Nikki didn't know what to make of all the information Torine was sharing in this drunken state. He was telling her information that she hadn't heard from him before. All this time, she was under the impression that he didn't have a relationship with his dad, but now she was intrigued to know what caused their relationship to fall apart. He never talked about him.

"I didn't know you used to be close with your dad, what happened with you two's relationship?" Nikki decided to outwardly ask Torine. Since he had been overly excited to talk, she thought why not, since it was harmless.

"He was too controlling and tried to control my life. I still hate the fact that I have his name. I should've changed it a long time ago," he responded. "Enough of him. I want to talk about how fine you are looking right now. Or how about how much I care about you. When we are done talking about that, we can talk about how much I can't wait to build a life with you. Then, we can talk about you sitting on my face and keeping me fed daily," he added with a big grin on his face before laughing.

"First off, I'm not cooking every day, so you can get that out…"

"Oh, I'm not talking about cooking," Torine interrupted Nikki while biting his bottom lip.

"Boooooy, why are you so nasty?" Nikki asked while giggling and play hitting Torine across the chest.

"It's only for you," He responded while smiling innocently.

When they made it back to the house, they both jumped out their shoes and plopped on the couch. Torine laid on Nikki until he fell asleep in between her legs.

"I wish you didn't have to leave tomorrow," Nikki said while kissing him on his forehead.

"Me too," he agreed and tossed his body to face the back of the couch. "We are a force when we are together." He finished before they both fell asleep.

~6~

The Dream

A few hours into her sleep, Nikki woke up from her slumber, except this time she wasn't waking up in her own bed. She was on a hard cot that felt like it was made of wooden planks with a feather-filled potato sack laid across the top, which was evident by the feathers floating in the air as Nikki scrambled to figure out where she was at.

She placed her hands-on top of her head in confusion of where she was, only to find her hair was braided into 6 individual plaits. This really freaked Nikki out, because her hair was normally in locs. She looked down at her clothes and she was wearing a worn-down dress, with white ruffles around the bottom. She didn't have anything on her feet and the floor was made of wooden planks with wide spaces to where you could see underneath.

"Where the hell am I?!" Nikki asked out loud.

"Shhhhh, be quiet fo' you make a scene," someone said from the far-left corner of the room. Nikki hadn't paid attention to the room because she was so focused on what she was wearing and what was *happening. As she looked around the room, she noticed there were four cots total in the room that was about 16x16 ft. in total size. On the right side of the room was a table set for two, with one chair and a spin wheel on the left side.*

Am I a slave? Nikki asked herself as she noticed the familiarity of the cabin in relationship to pictures and descriptions in books.

"Where am I?" Nikki asked the unknown woman.

"Whatchu mean? You sposed' tuh be sleep. Less you thinking bout doin something stupid?" The unknown woman asked, with their head tilted downward.

"No, no, I'm just asking because I woke up and noticed I was here. I was just sleeping with my boyfriend," Nikki responded. As soon as she finished, she realized how crazy she may have sounded to someone who didn't know who she was.

"Boyfriend? What's that you talkin' gurl?" The unknown woman asked.

Nikki realized at that moment, that she was dreaming and needed to get back to her regular life. Instead of continuing to respond to the unknown woman in the cabin, she decided to stop challenging it.

"Oh nothing, I'm about to lay back down," Nikki responded.

Nikki walked back to the cot where she woke up from, almost five minutes prior, and laid back down. She was laying there for almost five minutes when she heard yelling outside. Her cot was by a hole, that had a cloth covering over it, making it a window. Nikki raised her head to look outside the window and see what was happening.

"Aht aht, don't do that, less you ready to see almost anything," the mystery woman cautioned Nikki in a loud yet hushed voice.

Ignoring her warnings, Nikki took a look out the window and saw people being rushed out of their cabins. "What do you think happened?" She asked.

"It don't matter what happened, what matter is the fact that you then brought that bad juju in here, I told you don't...." -Before she could finish her sentence, a black man burst through the door ordering them to go outside into the courtyard.

"What's going on?" Nikki asked the man.

"Why are you questioning me? Do I need to pull out my whip?" He responded while reaching for his back pocket.

"No, no, I heard you," Nikki said, while scrambling to catch her composure. She looked around her cot for shoes to put on, before going outside, but there were none. She started to fret and talk to herself in her head. What is going on and where am I? She asked herself as she looked around for something to put on.

She had so many questions in her head that she was unable to answer.

"What's taking you so long?" The man asked while Nikki was looking around her cot. "Let's go, now!"

Nikki and the other woman from the cabin ran outside into the courtyard with over 100 other people. She looked around the crowd and noticed that everyone was dressed alike in a dark, dusty gray colored dress, knickers, or overalls. They appeared to be made out of potato sacks and inexpensive fabrics.

As she looked around and observed others in the crowd, everyone seemed to be confused as to what was happening. No one understood why it was so important to wake them up in the middle of the night.

"Masta Ramsey must really be upset at us about something," Someone behind Nikki said.

At that moment, Nikki heard someone yelling in the distance with a row of fire sticks marching behind it. It took a while for Nikki to make out what the person looked like and what they wanted, because they were coming from a dark area along the side of the cabins.

As they got closer, it looked like it was two white men pulling two black women by the necks with gags and collars. Nikki looked around to see if anyone else was as outraged as she was becoming. Just as she was about to yell out something, a voice yelled, "Stop!" Even though it sounded like it was said in a tone that everyone could hear it, Nikki soon realized that she was the only one who heard it.

She began wondering why she was experiencing what she was seeing and started questioning. All Nikki wanted to do was be back in her bed at home. As the men got closer with the women, Nikki overheard someone to the left of her talking to another.

"She healed Master Ramsey's boy, now he bout to hurt her. I don't get it," the lady said to the other *lady before starting to wail. Nikki turned around and looked at the crowd of people, with now over half of them crying.*

When they got close within eye reach, Nikki noticed they also had wooden stakes covering behind them. She started getting nervous, as she didn't understand what was going on and what was about to happen. As she noticed the two men pulling the women and stakes, she saw two other men behind them with torches raised high in the air. One of the women looked like she was slightly younger than the other.

Nikki didn't understand why she had to witness such a heinous crime being committed against Black women. It hit her in that moment, what the women said around her. They said it was Master Ramsey, which just so happened to be the same last name as the owner of Torine's family lineage. That made her want to started paying more attention to her surroundings.

By this time, every slave on the plantation was in the courtyard of the slave quarters. It had to had been nearing midnight- the time of night when the children should be sleeping peacefully and the adults praying for the sanctity of their existence. But no, everyone was in the middle of the courtyard witnessing two women be ridiculed amongst a couple hundred people at that point.

"This is what happens when you let the devil enter inside of you!" One of the men began to yell out loud. The ringing of his voice prompted everyone to turn and look his way.

"What is he talking about?" Nikki heard someone around her ask another person.

At this time, they had made their way into plain view and sight. Nikki could make out one of the women easily, as they were now standing under the light of the flames raised in the air, but the other one was hard to notice from the side Nikki was watching from. One of the women was short, with long plaits in her hair. The other woman looked older and her hair was also long and curly. What was interesting, is the fact that both of them had bright blue eyes from what Nikki could see.

Up until she met Sookani, Nikki had only met one other black woman with blue eyes, and that was Bibi. Bibi used to always talk about how she got her eyes from her grandmother. That was one of her favorite tales to share. Nikki started wondering why she didn't have blue eyes like Bibi and what it meant.

"Oh, that's Sophronia and Rose!" Nikki heard a woman shout behind her.

"Why are they in trouble? Specially with all the helpful stuff they do around here," Another woman chimed in the conversation.

Nikki was eaves dropping, to find out what was going on in the courtyard. Who was Sophronia and Rose? What did they do that was so important on the plantation? Nikki found herself with more and more questions as time went on.

"These nigger women think they are the Queen Mary or something," The man continued to talk in the background. "Let these women be an example for all you niggers who think they are equal to Hezues."

The man started reading stanzas from a handheld book he had. While he was reading, another man was setting up the stakes the women were dragging behind them. There were holes dug into the ground, for the stakes to be driven into.

"I heard they healed Massa's boy," The women continued talking behind Nikki.

"Such a shame, they try to help and end up getting killed. What we gonna do now? Now that our healers are shamed front uh everybody, who is gonna help now?" Another woman continued.

"Hezues healed the masses and saved us all from our sins. Before you two die tonight, I hope you repent." The man continued while his counterparts were fixing the stakes.

The crowd broke out in tears and loud cries. Anguished at the news, someone in the crowd cried out "noooooo!" Just as he started crying out loud, someone from the crowd, a black man, pulled out a whip and started hitting the man repeatedly.

"How dare you cry out against God and Masta's will?" He said while hitting the man.

Nikki felt the shift of energy in the courtyard as people watched the man be beaten, while they awaited the fate of Sophronia and Rose. It's as if the overseer beating the man forced everyone else to weep in silence. No one was brave enough to make a sound that was in any way familiar to an outcry or call against what was being witnessed in the courtyard. The energy of nervousness and fear spread across the crowd with each cackle of the flames.

"The devil thinks he is smarter than our God and Savior Lord Hezues, but not today. I have been given the power to put an end to the devil worshipping

*these niggers have been doing behind the sheds,"
Ramsey shouted out loud.*

*"Everything that is done in the dark will always
come to light!" He concluded.*

*At this time, the stakes were up, and the
women were being directed to stand on the foot
pedals attached to the wooden stakes. The women
stood on top of them, as they were then bound to the
stakes with a thick rope. Each man wrapped both
women until they were bound to the stakes like a
snake preparing to eat their prey. People in the
courtyard were fighting hard to keep their tears back
as they witnessed the preparation of the execution of
two of their peers.*

*"Ladies and gentlemen, these two negro women
thought they were God and took it upon themselves
to touch a white boy's body! To heal him. To heal
him from what? Now, my boy has to live the rest of
his life with the demon spirit inside of him that these
women put in him," he added.*

*As he finished talking, the other man was
almost done placing hay straw around the stakes that
each woman was placed on.*

"Tonight, you are going to witness what happens to Negro women who attempt to use magic here on this land," The man continued. "Are there any last words you two want to say to the people before you die tonight?"

The woman on the far left raised her head up to the sky and started speaking in an unknown language, "Ase bougheu duble erumunic erupinet serto vubertwain!"

Nikki looked around to see how the other people were reacting to her and if they understood what she was saying. It was an unknown language to her and from the looks of it, some people in the crowd knew what she was saying.

"What the creator put in me is in many more. You can't kill us all!" The lady continued to say, as her eyes lit up to a bright piercing cobalt blue, similar to the color of the midday sky. She moved her head around in circles and the glare of her eyes started lighting up every object it came in contact with.

"You see here, this is what happens when you allow the devil to possess you! No more, gimme that flame!" Ramsey demanded while snatching the torch out of another man's hand. He took it and set the hay, placed around the stakes, on fire.

Everyone watched as he set both stakes on fire. The women on the stakes didn't look afraid, surprisingly. They looked as if they were prepared to die. As the fire travelled up the stakes, the smell of burning flesh was starting to spread throughout the courtyard with dark smoke oscillating the air.

Nikki expected the women to start screaming and shouting as the flames took over their bodies, but they didn't. It was as if they were being consumed by the flames, but they were becoming the flames at the same time. As the flames rose to their head, the smoke coming from the fire started turning the same bright cobalt blue as her eyes.

Everyone looked into the sky in amazement and started screaming. No one knew what was going on as they were witnessing the flames change in front of them. One of the women kept her head down most of the time, making it hard for Nikki to make out her personal features. Nikki was dumbfounded because she didn't know if this was a real-life event or if her imagination was playing tricks on her in the dream state.

Nikki was still unsure of why she was witnessing this moment, but she was embracing it. At that moment, the room started spinning, and Nikki felt like she was entering a vortex. The speed of the room started going faster and faster and all of a sudden, a rainbow of colors blasted in the air and multi-colored paper confetti started falling all around her. She was traveling through an unknown vortex. She hadn't experienced this extremity in any of her previous dreams. All of a sudden, the room stopped spinning and all the gravity of the space returned. Nikki fell to the ground and landed on her head before the entire space turned pitch black.

Suddenly, Nikki woke up from her sleep breathing heavily. When she opened her eyes, she realized she was in her bed and no longer on the couch. Torine must've tucked them in sometime during the middle of the night. Surprisingly, she didn't remember it. Nikki rolled over to see if Torine was asleep, only to find him staring at her with a look of concern.

"Are you ok baby? You were tossing and turning," Torine asked.

"I just had a really intense dream and it felt like I was in it. I was on a slave plantation and saw these women get burned at the stake," she started talking. "The slave owner name was Ramsey, like the one you told me about yesterday," she finished; still breathing heavy.

"Ramsey? I don't remember telling you anything about anyone named Ramsey. I don't even think I know anyone named Ramsey. Who was he?" Torine asked while turning on his back and looking to the ceiling.

Confused at Torine's response, she rested on her elbow and responded, "Last night, you were telling me about a plantation owned by Ramsey that was passed down to your family."

"I don't remember saying any of that to you Baby, you have been having a lot going on, from the dreams to random outbursts, have you considered going to a therapist? I'm afraid that something might be wrong with you," he responded.

This was the last thing Nikki expected to hear him say to her. Did he not remember everything he said to her when he was in a drunken state the night before? How dare he try to make it seem like there was something wrong with her, when all she was trying to do was share what she was going through. Nikki found herself asking a bunch of questions over and over.

Do he think I'm crazy or something? Or is he crazy? What is he hiding? She started obsessing over what he had just told her. Nikki decided to not combat it and go with the flow. If she pushed it further, it was no telling what his response would be.

"Yea, you're right babe. Maybe I got the conversation confused with a movie or something. A lot has been going on since my birthday and I need to make sense of it all," She replied, while swinging her legs over the side of the bed to stand up.

"Your plane leaves later today, what would you like to do in the meantime?" Nikki asked Torine.

"First, I want you to serve me my favorite morning dish and then I want to talk about our future," he responded.

Interestingly enough, hearing him mention talking about futures made her cringe, because he had just left a bad taste in her mouth with the conversation they were having.

"Actually, I'm not really in the mood for sex right now," Nikki said to Torine as she grabbed her robe from the back of her bedroom door.

"How about I make you something to eat and then we can talk about the future?" Nikki asked, while tying her robe and leaning over to kiss Torine on the forehead before leaving out the room.

"Do I really have a choice?" Torine asked while laughing at the same time and turning to the other side of the bed.

Nikki went to the kitchen and prepared pancakes, eggs, and sausage for them to eat with orange juice on the side. While eating, they spent time talking about the future of their relationship, building a family and plans to get married. They even visited the idea of eloping at the courthouse when Nikki visited him again. Even though Nikki had a bitter taste in her mouth about Torine, she was slightly questioning if she was wrong for how she felt.

The couple spent the rest of Torine's time in Memphis together relaxing, talking, and eventually having sex. It was something about their sexual connection that Nikki couldn't let go of, even if he did rub her the wrong way with his words. Her coochie forgave him for her.

Nikki dropped Torine off at the airport a little before 8pm. He had a direct flight, so he was expected to make it home shortly after midnight. When they pulled up to the airport, they spent the next few minutes hugging each other and kissing goodbye before Nikki got back in the car and watched him walk away into the double doors leading into the airport lobby.

Remembering the envelope that Sookani gave her, Nikki looked down at the clock and saw she had a little less than 30 minutes left until she could open it. To rush time, she stopped at a vegetarian fast-food restaurant to grab something to eat. By doing that, she timed out her return home perfectly. She walked in the house at exactly 8:30pm and went straight to the couch to sit down while opening the envelope.

As she started opening the envelope, her heart was beating ridiculously fast. Something was telling her that she was opening a can of worms that she wouldn't be able to ever close again. The more she thought about it, Nikki decided to close the envelope and put it back in her purse. Something inside of her was telling her that she wasn't ready for what may be inside.

Instead of opening it as instructed, she decided to wait until the next day.

~7~

The Soul of The World

Exhausted by everything that had happened the few days before, all Nikki wanted to do was have a restful night of sleep. She found herself laying there for a couple of hours before she decided to open the envelope given to her by Sookani. *Maybe that's why I can't sleep,* she thought to herself.

Nikki rolled over and put on her glasses before getting up from her bed and retrieving her purse from the living room. She pulled the envelope out of her purse, sat down, and opened it. Inside of the envelope was a letter, a picture, and an article. As she pulled out the multi-paged letter, Nikki's heart started beating at how much was written. Instead of thinking too much, she unfolded the letter and started reading.

Dear Beloved Nikki,

> *You were born in a time that was not meant for you to exist in. Much of your life has been a lie passed down from generation to generation, stemming from when your ancestors were stolen and sold from our*

native lands. Do you know your ancestral roots? Do you know what countries your blood runs through?

My love, the stars have finally aligned for you to really learn who you are. You are Nia, One of The Seven Supreme Divinations of Inami. Everything that you have gone through, up until this point, was divinely guided for you to experience. Your lineage has been tainted and there are evil spirits ravaging inside the souls of people you know and people you don't know. These spirits carry the mission of demolishing our world of witchcraft and spirituality. Your mission has been unfolding in front of you this last year piece by piece. You may notice that your relationships have been changing and you have been attracting new people into your life. Nia, you are a witch with extensive healing powers inside of you.

When you turned 32, you unlocked the secrets of the universe, which was the night we met. The elders had been waiting for the chosen one to reveal themselves from your bloodline, and The Universe just so happened to reveal that it was you. You were meant to heal and bring balance back to the heart and history of our ancestors and land of Inami. The only way this can be done is by finding the Soul of The World and returning it to its rightful place. Back in 300 BC, someone by the name of Alamander, helped build the world's largest central place of study. People traveled from all over to visit this place in Africa, known as Kemeta, to learn about the stars, geometry, philosophy, mathematics, spirituality and so much more. This is where the Soul of The World was kept, In a hidden magical city right outside of Kemeta, known as Inami.

The Soul of The World is said to hold all the secrets to life, the future, and the all-seeing power of the creator. Alamander was the last known guardian to be seen with the Soul of The World and it was said that he hid it deep within a cave under the library he built. Around 290 BC, someone broke into the library and the caves in an attempt to retrieve the Soul of The World, which triggered an execution alarm.

The execution alarm set a bomb to the library. leaving the Soul of The World, and Alamander to never be seen again. What they didn't know is that Alamander was also among The Connectors which allowed him to place a spell on the Soul of The World, in preparation for an attack. The spell is said to have broken the Soul of The World into 7 *pieces and placed them in different parts of the world.*

Nia, the dream you had last night was placed there to show you where to start your journey. You are the chosen Nia to ensure the Soul of The World remains protected away from those who only want it for evil and power. The names mentioned in the dream were put there purposefully for you to pay attention to. You are never alone, your elder guides will be with you, but there will be things that only you will be able to do.

It is time for you to walk in your purpose and remember to always watch your back, because the same people who attacked Alamander for the Soul of the World had children, and their children had children who are hunting the chosen Supremes and The Soul of The World. The items included in this envelope should help you on your journey.

Nikki folded the letter up, put it back inside the envelope, and tossed the envelope on the floor next to her bed. She couldn't believe everything she had read and immediately questioned if she was going crazy. She had so many questions for what she had just read in the letter. What did Sookani mean by Supremes and the Soul of The World? What was harder for her, was feeling like she couldn't tell anyone about what she was experiencing. Would they even believe her?

She immediately started thinking about everything that had happened around the time of her birthday. All of the dreams she had been having that felt like real life experiences really stood out in her head. What was wracking the most havoc was the assumption that she was a witch. A divination witch, who is a part of a collective, to be exact.

For the next 30 minutes, Nikki went back and forth asking herself questions and re-reading the letter that was in the envelope. She had been so consumed with the letter that she didn't even think to look at the other items in the envelope. While wracking her brain, Nikki deep thought herself into a deep sleep.

For the first night in a long time, she didn't dream. She didn't drift into another dimension of time and experience. Instead, she was able to enjoy a long night's peaceful sleep without having to navigate the dreamworld. Nikki hadn't had the opportunity to experience something like this in quite some time, but for some reason, she was able to function as if she had been sleeping all night. Mentally, it was a totally different thing.

Nikki was sleeping so well, that she woke up late into the afternoon that Monday. By the time she woke up, the sun was raised high into the sky. There were no morning birds chirping, only dogs barking and music blaring like there was a community celebration going on outside. Only thing, there was no celebration. There was just Nikki lying on her back looking at the ceiling.

She was feeling and looking refreshed after finally getting a full night's sleep after so many nights of continuous dreaming. Wanting to take in the moment, Nikki laid there on her back for another 5 minutes, attempting to not think about the night before. Unfortunately, she was unable to block out what she read in the envelope Sookani gave her.

As soon as Nikki thought about the letter, it hit her that she hadn't looked at the other contents in the envelope. She was so focused on the letter and trying to understand what she had read, that she didn't realize she may have been missing some important information.

Nikki laid there questioning if she should look at the remaining contents in the envelope. She rolled over to her side to retrieve her phone and noticed that Torine texted her to let her know when he made it home the night before. She responded to his message with a heart reaction and locked her screen.

With her legs dangling along the side of the bed, she looked around her bed for her house shoes before standing up. After she put her house shoes on, she grabbed her robe from behind the room door, put it on, and made her way to the bathroom. When Nikki made it into the bathroom, she turned on the lights and looked in the mirror for about 60 seconds, before she sat on the toilet and placed her head in her hands.

So much had happened, that she no longer knew how to define reality from fantasy. She read about supernatural things in books, but she never thought it would happen directly to her. She realized the more that happened to her, the less she could communicate with other people about the experiences. She knew there were some people who would go so far as to get her committed into a mental institution. As Nikki thought about who she could call and talk to, Arieka was the only person that came to mind.

She always felt like Arieka was quirky and slightly weird just like her. If there was someone who wouldn't judge her, it would be her. Instead of calling, Nikki decided she was going to figure everything out on her own. Even with Sookani, Nikki still felt uneasy about what she was experiencing.

Not only did Nikki want to investigate everything in regard to the content in the envelope, but she also had to do some work for her personal life. She needed to do market research for her business, look at her budget for May, and draft material to record for Flixzit. A lot had been going on in the most recent past weeks for Nikki. Her shipment was delayed, and she was preparing to relaunch her cosmetic company after going through a rebranding process, which was expensive in itself.

As much as Nikki wanted to explore the contents of the envelope, she knew she needed to handle business first. She hadn't really touched on her business work the entire weekend while Torine was visiting, which wasn't good because she hadn't been keeping up with her content. From recording for Flixzit, finishing the school semester, and rebranding her business it was becoming a lot to handle. It was a given, if she looked at the envelope first, she wouldn't get to her other work that needed to be done for her to pay her bills.

Nikki spent the next few hours researching market trends, color codes, and brainstorming branding ideas. She hadn't even gotten to planning her Flixzit content before she found her anxiety getting the best of her. Besides her having to redirect herself to stay on track every five minutes, she could no longer hold it in. Her mind had been wandering back and forth to the envelope and letter.

Flashes of the scratchy texture, of the letter, had been popping into Nikki's head randomly all day. As she felt herself holding the letter and reading it over and over, her heart started beating faster. Was she nervous? Or was she anxious in fear of the road she was heading down. The letter was basically telling her that she was destined to be a superpowered superhuman. You don't see many Black Women in that role.

Just at the beginning of the year, Nikki was embracing life and celebrating her freedom and peace away from people. Now, just almost 5 months later, life looked totally different from what was planned and expected. Not only was she in a new relationship, but her business took a major hit, the country went into a lockdown, and she found out she was some sort of witch. It was constantly taking Nikki for a loop, whenever she thought about everything that had been happening.

If she told the wrong people about what she had been experiencing, she was sure they would try to have her committed to therapy or a psychiatric hospital. How would she sound, telling them she teleported to another place and some mysterious woman gave her a letter telling her that she was meant to save the world from destruction? She would sound like a lunatic if that information fell on the wrong ears.

Nikki was sitting there thinking about what to do. She didn't feel comfortable going down the journey and road alone. She needed support, she needed someone to turn to if she ever got lost or needed to talk to someone. The more she thought, she realized that Arieka was the only person she could talk to. She debated back and forth between telling her, but she needed to talk to someone. She had no planned speech, she was just going to let it out.

As the phone rang, she felt the sweat beading up along her forehead hairline. She didn't know how Arieka would respond, but something was telling her that it would be a safe space.

"Hey girl, heeeey!" Arieka answered the phone excitedly.

"Heeeeeey Girl! How are you?" Nikki asked.

"I'm doing ok, same ole same old, working on getting this business plan together," Arieka responded.

"Ayyyye, Periodt! I'm so happy for you! How is it going?" Nikki asked excitedly.

"Getting on my nerves honestly, so let's just not even talk about it. How are you?" Arieka responded.

"I see what you just did there. You're lucky I was calling you because I wanted to talk about me," Nikki said laughing, "Life has been crazy as hell huntyyyy and whew!" she finished dramatically.

"Girllll, What the hell is going on with you?" Arieka asked Nikki bluntly.

Without thinking, Nikki blurted out, "Long story short, I think I'm a witch."

"Well, alrighty then, where did that come from chica?" Arieka asked confused.

"Girl, so much stuff has happened since the last time we talked for real. Like, even when we talked on my birthday, I had just experienced some weird shit. Soooo, before I tell you this, you aren't going to think I'm crazy, are you? Because I don't need anyone trying to have me committed into an institution," Nikki responded nervously. She knew Arieka wouldn't do something like that, she just wanted to make sure twice.

Rolling her eyes in the back of her head, Arieka responded back, "Girl, don't play with me. What the fuck you got going on down there? Do I need to help you get rid of a body or something?"

"Nah, it ain't that bad. But girllllll This lady appeared to me while Torine was visiting and she gave me a letter to read. This letter went into a place called Inami, and how I am the descendent of powerful women. I've been having hella dreams where I am an active participant and not just in a vivid daydream. In one of them, I was actually a

140

slave and I had to watch 2 black women be burned at the stake for being alleged witches. Girl it's been so much. In the envelope she gave me it had the letter, a picture and a news article." Nikki rambled.

"Oh, that is a lot! What was it a picture of? How do you feel about everything?" Arieka asked while straightening her sitting posture.

"I really don't know how to look at it. A big part of me thinks it is real. Especially, since I have been experiencing some supernatural things within my life and dreams. Maybe I'm just looking for someone to tell me I'm not crazy," she responded with her voice tone lowering with each syllable spoken.

Nikki and Arieka talked for another hour discussing everything that had been going on with Nikki, which was a big place of comfort for her. She was able to share her dreams, interactions with Sookani, and her feelings regarding Torine. It was still concerning Nikki that Torine had become defensive when he learned that he revealed information about his family when he was drunk. She started questioning why he reacted the way he did. Was he hiding something? Was he one of the bad people Sookani warned her about? So many thoughts began to roam in her mind, and she used this time to let it all out to Arieka. Even with the threat of danger nearing, Nikki felt she could trust her with everything.

The conversation ended with Arieka suggesting that Nikki look through the rest of the envelope when she got the chance to relax in her bed. The last thing she wanted Nikki to go through was the feeling of being alone and weird. So, she used that time to listen to Nikki and be a support. Nikki got off the phone feeling confident in the journey she was about to take. Her nervousness and anxiety had ceased, and she was ready to open the can of worms.

Nikki took the next hour to shower, make something to eat, and smoke a joint to prepare herself for the information she was about to dive into. Before getting in the bed, she grabbed the envelope that was tossed on the floor the night before, out of anxiety mixed with a large amount of confusion.

As she jumped in the bed, she pulled the blanket back to climb under it. She placed her phone on the side of her and held the envelope in her other hand as she pulled the covers over her legs. Nikki held the envelope in her hand, looked at it, and took a deep breath before opening.

She opened the envelope, closed her eyes, and pulled out the first thing her fingers landed on. Nikki knew before she had the item out of the envelope, that it was a picture. As Nikki pulled the picture out the envelope her heart started beating faster and faster as if it was going to explode out of her chest. She flipped it over and couldn't believe her eyes. It was a picture of Bibi when she was younger. Nikki was able to easily identify her because she remembered seeing other pictures of Bibi when she was growing up.

Also in the picture was Bibi's mom Sylvia, what looked like her mom Sophia, and two other women she didn't know. The two mysterious women were all older than the other women in the picture. The more Nikki stared at the picture, the more she felt there was something hidden in meaning. She couldn't figure out what it was exactly, which made her stare at the picture even more. The pose of the picture looked eerily similar to the picture she had of herself, Bibi, Grandma Sylvia, and her great aunt Lula at the grave of Grandma Sophia.

The thought of this made her jump up from the bed to go grab the picture from the grave site. She ran to the living room to grab it from the cubicle bookshelf in the corner. She rummaged from shelf to shelf looking for the picture but couldn't find it. She stopped, put her hands on her hips and looked around the room trying to remember where she put the picture.

Nikki ran into her office space to grab her photo book. She flipped through the pages restlessly, looking for the picture. When she got to the final page, she found that the picture wasn't in the picture book either. This was starting to frustrate Nikki, the more she was unable to locate the picture. Nikki got quite frustrated.

All of a sudden, a voice said to her, "It's in your room on the dresser under the card located in the left corner of your dresser."

Nikki looked around as she listened to the voice talking to her. This was the first time something like this had ever happened to her. Usually when there was a voice of reason present, attempting to get her attention, it sounded like her own voice. But not this time though. This time, it was the voice of an older woman who was welcoming you into her home for the first time with a home cooked meal.

She decided to not question the voice and walked to her bedroom. She made it to her room and looked in the exact spot the voice told her. Low and behold, Nikki found the picture sitting there. She immediately got excited and thanked the mysterious voice that told her where to look.

She grabbed the picture and jumped back in her bed to compare the pictures. She wanted to focus on finding things she hadn't noticed before. She thought back to the day when they took the picture. Nikki was really young, but she remembered she was with Bibi the whole time. They went to the church for a while, went to the grave, and then they went to a meeting with a bunch of other women. That was all she could remember as she was trying to put the pieces together and make sense of it all.

Nikki now had both pictures in her hands, and she found herself looking back and forth from one picture to the next. Within a couple minutes of analyzing the pictures and each person, Nikki noticed a symbol that was in both pictures. It was on all of their clothes in both pictures. The symbol looked like an upside-down capitalized Y with an S intertwined. For some reason she hadn't noticed it's discreet placement on the bottom of their dresses. The only reason why Nikki noticed it this time was probably because she was looking for something to drastically stand out.

Now that the symbols were becoming so evident, Nikki found herself becoming more intrigued by everything that had been going on. Were they in a secret society? What did the symbol mean? What was she supposed to be finding out? Nikki found herself having so many questions and lacked answers to all of them.

She grabbed the envelope and pulled out the news article that was inside. She pulled it out so fast, that a part of the paper ripped. Thankfully, it was still readable. Written across the top of the page, in capital letters, were the words: TWO NIGGER WITCHES BURNED YESTERDAY!

Nikki's eyes lit up, because she automatically thought back to her dream from the other night when she witnessed two black women burned at the stakes for allegedly healing their master's son from an ailment. As she started reading the article, she realized it was indeed talking about the same incident from her dream. This article looked like a reprint photocopy of the original article as it was printed on newer paper, and you could see the scanned paper outline.

The article, dated 1963, began reading:

> *Two negro girls were burned at the stake last night to show that we must not disobey God or practice witchcraft, as it is from the devil. Chairs, get your slaves in order so this doesn't have to happen to you. Next thing you know, they will be casting spells and killing all of us even when they should be thanking us.*
>
> *If you need any help educating your slaves, come to the community meeting that will be held on the 10th day of June at the Westend Farmer Mill at 6 o'clock.*

Under the original print, there were some notes that were hard to make out, signed by someone named John Ceemore. Nikki was slightly shaken up as she found herself spinning out and having a flashback to the dream. The flashback went immediately to when Nikki was watching the women on the stakes. This time, it zoomed in and was focused on their clothing, and there, she saw sewn on the woman's dress was the same symbol she saw on their clothes in the pictures.

Nikki threw the pictures down on the bed and scooted backwards.

What the fuck is going on right now?- She began to panic.

Nikki kept going back and forth mentally, trying to make sense of all the information she had just stumbled upon. What had been bugging her the most was how Sookani got a copy of the picture and the article reprint. Both of the items were from quite some time ago and only someone who was truly divinely connected could find them and get them to her. The more Nikki thought about everything that was going on, the more she connected with the idea of her potentially being a real witch, like Sookani said.

She reached for the article again and analyzed it. The reprint author's name stood out to Nikki which gave her the idea to attempt reaching out to him for more information. Not thinking about how crazy it may sound emailing him, Nikki was determined to get more information regarding all of the content she had taken in the last 24 hours.

Nikki reached across her body to grab her phone. She unlocked the screen and opened her internet browser to begin searching for the article's owner. As a result of searching the words "John Ceemore Slave Article," she became aware that there was more than one John Ceemore who wrote an article on slavery. This brought her to the reality that it may be harder than she thought, at first.

She clicked on the first result and began reading about a John Ceemore who was located in New Orleans. He was known for covering old slave tales and news of slave revolts and push back against their oppressors. The website also included a list of articles that he was known for. Nikki scanned the list of articles looking for one labeled: TWO NIGGER WITCHES BURNED YESTERDAY!

She didn't see any titles that looked remotely familiar, which made her develop an inkling inside that this wasn't the journalist she was looking for. Nikki went back to the search bar and changed her search to "John Ceemore Two Nigger Witches," and she was amazed by all the website results that showed up. She clicked on the first one and started reading.

The website was called Journal Rejexxx which was a very intriguing name for a website brand. Instead of reading the page regarding Mr. Ceemore, Nikki read the about section of the website. As she scanned the about page on the site, she realized that all the journalists that were listed on the website were deemed rejects in the journalism world. Some of them were black-balled from the industry for reasons spanning from lying in their work to releasing information that made the wrong people mad. This made her nervous, slightly, but she decided to continue.

She went back to the page with the information on John Ceemore and scrolled through the page to see the titles and headlines listed. In his description, it said that he was a part of the journal Rejexxx because he was known for releasing esoteric information and allegedly fabricating pieces of information at the same time. This intrigued Nikki because it made her wonder what information he released that wasn't supposed to be known to others more than what he lied about.

After looking through his information on the site, she looked at the tab labeled "popular works," and the third item on the list was the article she was looking for. There wasn't any extra information available outside of the reprint that looked exactly like the copy Nikki had. She got a little suspicious and questioned if Sookani got a copy of the article from off the internet.

After reading through the article again and scanning the other articles listed as well, Nikki realized the only way she would be able to get the information she was looking for would be from reaching out to John Ceemore herself. As crazy as it sounded, it felt like the best option for her, if she wanted to get to the bottom of all the new information that had been brought to her attention. Reaching out to John Ceemore was her passport to the next level on her journey. She started hunting through the page for John's contact information, but she was unable to find it on the website.

She went to her internet search bar and typed his name again, but this time she added a city behind it. She found from the most recent two articles on the website that he had transitioned to San Diego, California where he was researching the platonic shift that was projected to hit California in 2050, forcing it to become an island and no longer a part of the 48 continuous states in the United States of America.

After adding the word 'city' she also typed in the word 'email' to trigger the search to give his contact information. The first page that came up, was his professional page on Link Me In, which is a networking site for professionals of all backgrounds. Unfortunately, his page was locked, so Nikki was unable to see any information outside of the "message me" button. She felt it would be weird to add him as a contact, since they hadn't had any mutual connections. Since she was unable to see a personal email, she made the decision to send him a direct message from her Link Me In account and hope for the best. Not knowing what to say or where to even begin, Nikki started typing:

Hello Mr. Ceemore,

My name is Nikki, and I came across your article that was a reprint of the burning of two black slave girls in Carolina. I was wondering if we could chat sometime to discuss the incident and what made you bring it back to the surface. I really enjoyed finding the excerpt and I would love to talk to you and see how we can work together. Thank you.

When she finished writing, she hit send before even thinking about what she wrote or attempting to edit it. Thankfully, there was no way to delete sent messages and it was out there now. It was her only hope that he didn't think she was crazy.

Nikki found herself going back and forth between if she should send another message to clarify what she was asking or if she should just wait to see if he responded to the first message. She decided to wait for him to respond, so she didn't look like a desperate creep, especially since it was later in the evening time and everything was timestamped. If she sent a follow-up message, it would be showing a few minutes after the original message, which could make it look like she didn't really know what she wanted.

There was nothing more she could do but wait for him to get back to her when he could. In the meantime, Nikki went back and read the letter from Sookani again. There was a line that stood out to her this time:

> *Do you know your ancestral roots? Do you know what countries your blood runs through?*

Interestingly enough, Nikki had already been wondering how far her DNA extended and what countries she was related to. *Maybe it's time for me to do a DNA test,* she thought to herself as she searched for the best company to work with. There was a website called African Blood, that was dedicated to helping people from the African Diaspora find their bloodlines. Just her luck, they were running a sale for 50% off for a limited time.

After reading a few reviews, of the company, Nikki looked up a few videos on Flixzit of others sharing their experience with finding out their roots and countries they were connected to. She found herself convinced after less than an hour of research. She ordered the test for $99 and felt satisfied with the direction she was going in. The payment instructions stated it would take 2-3 business days for her to receive her test kit in the mail. Once she got the kit in the mail, she was instructed to send it back in the self-addressed packaging. She could send it back the same day, depending on time she received it. After sending the sample back, they said results are made available in 2-3 weeks on the online portal.

It had been a long day for Nikki, so she decided to get ready for bed. She laid her phone on the bed next to her and took a deep sigh. Nikki got up to turn the lights off before getting back in the bed to drift off to sleep. Unfortunately, her mind had other plans at the moment. After laying there, looking at the ceiling for almost 15 minutes, Nikki got up and rolled a joint to help her relax her mind and body. After smoking half the joint, Nikki laid back down and fell into a deep sleep.

As soon as she fell asleep, she found herself in a foreign land. In this land, she was surrounded by pyramids on all sides. There were people flying in the air with no wings and mystical looking creatures walking the land. She seemed to be the only regular human there and it didn't look like they knew she was there. She was simply a bystander taking in the beauty of this mysterious place.

The sky was a colored mixture of blue, purple, pink, yellow, and green that looked like a kindergarten classroom had been playing in watercolors. It was beyond beautiful to look at, as Nikki found herself in a daze looking around her. She had a happy feeling running through her entire body, as she found herself wondering if she was in heaven. She remembered hearing stories of heaven since she was a little girl and that was how she imagined it to be.

This had to be the same place she was raised to aspire for. Nikki walked around this magical place she was experiencing in awe. There were buildings, mystical people and creatures engaging each other, and children playing outside with strange toys. As the young children were playing, some of them would jump up and drift down like a feather on a warm day. The whole place had a happy vibe.

Nikki walked around a little more and discovered an alleyway that was dark. Something told her to walk down the alley and see what she would find, even though she no longer had the happy positive feelings inside of her as just a couple moments prior. Shortly after she began walking down the alley, she came across the entrance to a pub that looked old and worn down. Before walking in, she looked in the window and she noticed Sookani sitting at a table with a man. It looked like they were in the middle of a heated discussion, as he slammed his fist down on the table.

Nikki opened the door to the pub and walked in. As soon as she walked in, the entire pub turned to look at her. It wasn't like outside, where it seemed as if no one knew who she was and made it seem as if she didn't exist. The pub had a gloomy vibe to it, everything was colored a rusty gray, and it looked nothing like outside. Nikki looked over towards the table where Sookani and the man were sitting and proceeded to walk their way. As she started walking their way, the man got up from the table and stormed out of the building. While passing Nikki, she was able to get a small glimpse of his face that was hidden beneath his cloaked robe that was a shiny onyx color. She was able to make out a scar that spanned from his left ear to the bottom right of his chin.

"You made it my love!" Sookani said to Nikki, waving for her to come to the table and join her as she stood up.

"Welcome to the Pub of Truth and Vision!" Sookani continued with her greeting. "Here, nothing can be hidden, and everything seen isn't pretty," she said to Nikki as she sat back down motioning for Nikki to sit.

"Why am I here?" Nikki asked.

"Well, my darling, you are here because it is time for you to begin learning your history. I'm proud of the work you have been doing, keep going," Sookani answered Nikki while stirring her hot drink. "It's time for you to learn who you are and where you came from. That is why your dream brought you here, your heart is officially opened and ready to receive everything the universe and your ancestors have been waiting to give you." She continued.

"So, what should I do next? Can you tell me about the picture and article that was in the envelope you gave me?" Nikki asked.

"Your heart knows the way and there is only so much that I can help you with. Have faith and trust that you are on the right path my darling. You are divinely connected," Sookani responded.

As soon as Sookani responded to Nikki the dream stopped. Nikki was now in a dark room with a bed and nothing else. Something in her told her to get in the bed and lay down, which is what she did. After she got in the bed, she felt herself falling asleep again, inside of the dream.

Needless to say, she got some of the best sleep that night. Which was exactly what she needed, in order to prepare for all of the work that was coming to her in the near future. This was only the beginning and something in Nikki's spirit told her it wasn't going to be an easy one.

~8~

Connecting the dots

A little over 1 month had passed since Nikki started researching the contents of the envelope, she got from Sookani. It was now the first week of June and it was definitely beginning to look and feel like summer outside. The children were outside playing while their parents watched them and tended to their personal yard spaces. Birds were chirping songs of love and happiness as they flew from tree to tree to mingle with each other.

Everything was flowing and Nikki was in a good mood. She was preparing orders for her business. Since its relaunch, she had been super busy with everything, which was a good thing. Her DNA test results hadn't come in yet and she was still anxiously waiting on them along with a response from Mr. Ceemore. Many would think she was irate by how long she had been waiting, without reaching out again, but something told her to just wait a little longer. Her business kept her from thinking too much on the extended time it was taking for her to get more information regarding everything that had been unfolding.

It was around 12noon, on a Monday, when Nikki took a quick break from working to check her emails. When she opened her inbox, she saw a message from Link Me In stating she had a new message in her inbox. She automatically assumed it was John Ceemore because she hadn't been in conversation with anyone else on the application since she last logged in to send him the message. It had to be him responding back to her, finally!

Nikki rushed to her inbox, and just as she intuitively thought, it was a message from Mr. Ceemore. She immediately got anxious and nervous regarding what his message was going to say. She was afraid to open it too soon- leaving her without a response. She didn't want to leave him on read.

Nikki found herself analyzing the entire situation for almost 5 minutes before finally opening the message to see his response. It wasn't a 2-sentence response like Nikki was expecting for sure, which made her smile as she took a glimpse at the preview of the message before clicking:

> *Nikki, thank you for reaching out to me in regard to my reprint of said article. That reprint was a passion project for me that to..*

She was hooked at the preview and intrigued by what all he had to say to her. She took 3 deep breaths in and out before opening the message. To her surprise it wasn't as many words as she was expecting, which made her excitement tone down a few levels. She took a deep breath and started reading.

> *Nikki, thank you for reaching out to me in regard to my reprint of said article. That reprint was a passion project for me that took some time to put together. If you are reaching out to me, then it means you may be on a journey to finding the truth about the true history of this Country. I would love to talk more about the article if you're interested. Feel free to give me a call at 555-034-7222 to discuss more. I hope I can be of assistance to you.*

Nikki read the message three times before snapping out of the slight daze she had found herself in. Not only was he willing to help her, but he was also willing to give her a phone number to call and speak. Nikki wondered why he chose to not communicate over the messenger. She had waited a long time for him to respond to her message, and found herself blaming self for not asking clear and concise questions in the original message.

In that moment, she remembered that he gave her his phone number to communicate further, which could be a good thing. Nikki looked over at the time and saw it was after noon which was typically considered lunch-time in much of the time zone. She decided that it was the perfect time to call Mr. Ceemore and have the discussion. As soon as she opened the phone app, it hit her that she needed to make an outline of what she wanted to say and ask Mr. Ceemore. She didn't want to make it seem like she was wasting time and she wanted to make sure that she got as much information she could from him.

She ran to her office space to grab paper and a pen and made her way to her bedroom and hopped in the bed. Nikki began making a list of questions she wanted to ask Mr. Ceemore while sitting with her legs crossed. She knew she wanted to ask him how he got the article. She also wanted to ask him if he knew the slave owners and the names of the slaves. There were quite a few things she wanted to ask him, and she wanted to make sure she got the most important questions first before his time ran out.

For the next 5 minutes, Nikki wrote down a list of questions she wanted to ask Mr. Ceemore. Her heart started beating fast as she got anxious thinking about how the conversation would go. What would he be like? Would he be helpful? Was he an ally? Did he know Sookani too? She had so many thoughts and questions that needed to be answered.

Nikki picked up her phone again, but this time it was to actually make the phone call. She went to her messages and clicked on the phone number in the conversation. By clicking on the number, it prompted the phone to dial out. The phone rang 3 times before an older man answered.

"Hello!" The man answered the phone with enthusiasm in his voice. His voice was deep with a little bit of a raspy tone to it.

"Hello, this is Nikki, can I speak to Mr. Ceemore?" she responded.

"Well, this is him. How are you doing?" Mr. Ceemore asked cheerfully.

"I'm doing well, I am the woman who messaged you on Link Me In," she responded.

"Oh, I know exactly who you are. I don't give my phone number out to anyone these days. There are too many people who are out to prey on old people like me, so I try to stay away as much as possible. It was something about your message that drew my attention. Something told me I needed to talk to you," Mr. Ceemore said.

Nikki got more comfortable the more he talked. *What was it about me that made him feel comfortable?* Nikki thought to herself.

"Now, I know you were reaching out to me about my reprint article of those slave girls that were burnt on the stake. When I did that article, it was something that I just so happened to stumble across when I started at The Andiko. I was a young lad, fresh out of journalism school. I was able to snab an internship with one of the top editors at the company. It was almost unheard of!" Mr. Ceemore continued.

While Mr. Ceemore was talking, it became clear that most of Nikki's questions were going to be answered from his introduction.

"So, one month into working for him, I was given the assignment to find content material that would cause a stir and get people to talkin'. It was the last quarter of the 1963 fiscal year, and they wanted to go out with a bang. The success of my article was a determining factor in whether I would be considered to be hired as full-time when my internship expired. That was really important because there weren't any newspapers looking to hire a colored man. I'm not talking too much about myself, am I?" Mr. Ceemore stopped to ask Nikki.

"Oh, no. You're perfectly fine. I'm just listening and taking in the information," Nikki responded back in admiration.

"I just have to make sure, cause I'm an old guy and old guys can sometimes talk too much." Mr. Ceemore continued talking with a chuckle. "So, it was a cold Boston night, and I was looking through some old papers in my apartment to get an idea of what type of article I wanted to do. I had to have been looking at old articles for almost 16 hours before I got frustrated and decided to take my talents to the nearest pub," he added with a severe laugh. He laughed so hard, that he gave off a grunt.

"So, I went to the pub that was up the street from my house, Jummy's. By this time, I'm a regular and they all knew my name and what I liked to drink. As always, the bartender gave me the first drink on the house. But something different happened this time. Right when I was finishing my first drink, the bartender brought me another drink before I had a chance to order. I was confused because he had never done that before. So, I asked him what the drink was for. He told me that it was already paid for by the lady at the end of the bar," Mr. Ceemore stopped.

Nikki found herself getting more intrigued into the conversation and how he came about the article. Even though it seemed like he was giving irrelevant information, something about it made her feel like she should be listening to what he was saying. Because of this, she didn't interrupt him. Even though he took such a long pause.

"So, I look down at the end of the bar and I see this gorgeous dark-skinned black woman dressed in all black. I'll never forget her because she had red eyes and they were piercing like the reflection of blood in a glass reflecting light from the room," Mr. Ceemore continued in an exciting tone.

Nikki found herself getting more intrigued by the story, especially after he mentioned the mysterious woman with red eyes. Up until that day, she had only seen 1 black women with red eyes and that was Sookani when she first met her.

"Can you tell me more about the woman?" Nikki asked. Something in her felt like he would be revealing the information soon enough during the conversation.

"She was so beautiful, and I will never forget her, even though she never gave me her name," Mr. Ceemore said with a little hesitation and guilt in his voice.

"Anywho, she sent me a drink and I looked her way and nodded. This was the first time a lady had ever sent me a drink, so I was a little thrown off on what to do. I was a man, so I didn't want to look like a hissy and not approach the situation right. So, instead of saying anything to her, I let her come to me. Interestingly, she didn't come to me after that second drink. She actually bought me 3 more drinks before she finally came and sat next to me. By this time, I was feeling really good and I felt like she was trying to take advantage of me if you know what I mean," Mr. Ceemore said with a giggle. It sounded like he wished to live his younger days again.

"I feel like I'm talking your ear off now, So I'm going to make the rest of it much shorter. She came and sat by me and asked me about myself and what I did for a living. She told me that she had seen me many times before, but she was afraid to tell me. We spent the next 10 minutes talking about my job, she seemed so intrigued that I didn't think to ask her about her life and what she did for a living. But that's how the tables turned, so I can't cry over that spilled milk. When she was ready to go, she gave me one of the tightest hugs I had ever encountered and that was that. I finished off my last drink and made my way home upset that I was going home alone. Don't judge me young lady." He added.

"Since I was going home alone, I was planning to do more research work to identify the article topic I wanted to do. Before hanging my coat on the door rack, I reached in my jacket pockets to clean them out and I found something interesting," Mr. Ceemore stated. "It was an original newspaper press that was dated June 1, 1861, to the article you messaged me about. The article talked about a witch burning that took place two days prior on one of the largest plantations. From my research, the article spread through North Carolina in a matter of one week and it made its way to the New England territories at some point as well. It was always strange to me how the article got in my pocket. Until this day, I believe it was that beautiful woman I had the pleasure of meeting at the pub that day." He finished.

Nikki saw this as the perfect opportunity to jump into the conversation with some follow-up questions. He already answered a lot of the questions she had on her paper with his introduction, but there were still more questions that she had.

"What made you turn it into a reprint?" Nikki asked.

"Well, honestly, when I think back I only did it because I knew it would lead me to my full-time position that I ended up not getting anyways," he answered.

Nikki took in his response and realized he wasn't emotionally invested in the story, which let her know that he didn't know much past the facts of the article and case. Even though she was beginning to believe that it was Sookani who gave him the article to print, she felt she wouldn't make much of a difference by bringing her up.

"Can you tell me anything about the slave owner?" Nikki asked in response.

"So, what I found is that he was a pretty harsh man, Jim Ramsey, he was known for being one of the hardest. He was especially harsh on the black women and girls. I learned through my research that he felt that many of the black women were possessed with evil that allowed them to do supernatural things. There was a time when his crop was unable to yield as much as they needed to make for the season, so he blamed the women and ordered to have all of them beaten until someone confessed to Conjuring a spell against him. He would then have them burned at the stake for everyone to watch." Mr. Ceemore answered before pausing. "What led you to start researching the article?" He asked.

"I came across the article randomly and it intrigued me. I'm currently doing research on the American slave trade and I wanted to learn more historical information that I hadn't been aware of prior to." Nikki lied.

"Oh, so you're a scholar. We need more of those around here these days. It seems like nowadays everyone just wants to play games and go to the disco lounge to party," He responded. The sound of his voice showed that he was not a fan of the changing times. He was a simple and traditional man and it showed through his use of words and tone. At that time, Nikki only had one more question that she wanted to ask during the conversation. She had taken in everything he shared with her and it was an overwhelming amount of information that she had to work through.

"So, I think I have one more question for you, if that's ok?" Nikki asked.

"Shoot," he responded.

"Were you ever able to find the names of the slave women who were burned in that article?" Nikki asked nervously. As she finished asking the question, her body started sweating profusely, and she was unable to stop it. It felt like her body temperature jumped at least 10 degrees as soon as the hot flashes started. She was nervous to he what he was going to say. Did he know the women? And if he did, where would that take her in her search?

There were so many questions going through Nikki's head at once.

"Interestingly enough, I was able to find the names for both of them after I put out a call for information. Their names were Sophronia Kipper and Rose Sumpter. Sophronia was Rose's best friend while they were on the plantation. They were known for being the plantation medicine mothers. They both had children who were set free in 1865. Sophronia's daughter Binta later married Jimmy Soldent. Rose, she had a son named Bobby Sumpter. Bobby later got married to Virginia and they began their lineage." Mr. Ceemore answered.

Nikki was in a daze after listening to what Mr. Ceemore had just said. She couldn't believe that this entire time, it was her Great Great Great Great grandmother's death that she witnessed firsthand. It was that moment, when she realized why Sookani sent her on this witch hunt. She wanted Nikki to find it out for herself that she was from a lineage of slaves who had magical powers within them. But who was that other woman who was killed at the stakes with her? Nikki felt a strong desire to learn more about her as well.

"You still there?" Mr. Ceemore asked Nikki after it went into an awkward silence.

"Oh yea, sorry about that. I'm just trying to make sure I don't mess up any notes from everything you shared here today. I am so appreciative of everything you took the time to share with me today," Nikki responded. "Would it be ok for me to call you in the future if I ever have any more questions?" Nikki asked.

"Oh yea, that is perfectly fine. I personally enjoyed this conversation we had today. It's not every day that an old man gets the opportunity to talk to a young pretty girl such as yourself." He answered.

Nikki saw that as the perfect time to get off the phone and finish her research with the new information that had been given to her. She had become too anxious to remain on the phone a minute longer.

"I am really grateful for everything you have shared today. I will definitely be reaching out if I feel there is more I would like to learn," Nikki added.

"Oh definitely, I have other black slave stories to talk about as well if you're interested," He offered.

"I will definitely contact you in the future," Nikki responded, now rushing Mr. Ceemore off the phone.

Not only was she sensing him flirting with her, but she was also ready to dive into all of the new information she had just learned.

When the call ended, Nikki threw her phone on the bed next to her and laid back on her pillow. As she laid there on her back, she looked up at the ceiling and started daydreaming. The daydream went from her being on the slave plantation, to her being at one of her family reunions. As soon as she snapped out of it, she found herself staring at the pictures and notes from the conversation she just had with Mr. Ceemore.

Nikki didn't know if she wanted to keep researching or if she wanted to take a break and think about all the information she had to decipher through. She set the pictures down and started looking up at the room ceiling. As she laid there looking at the ceiling, all of a sudden, she felt her body begin to lift off the bed. She didn't notice it immediately; it was only after she thought the room was moving and panicked. Her body was about 6 inches off the bed before she started panicking and fell back onto the bed.

Nikki didn't know what had just happened. She read about people floating before and remembered seeing the flying people in her dream. Even though she'd seen it before, she hadn't thought it would be something she would experience personally.

She pulled out her phone and started searching for information regarding floating in the air. Shortly after beginning her search she regretted the decision. It left her more confused than before. After almost an hour of intense searching online and reading articles, Nikki had thought herself into exhaustion and felt a nap was her best option before she jumped into working on something different. Most times, Nikki found herself needing to take a puff of a joint to calm her nerves to fall asleep, but not this time. She was asleep and snoring in less than 2 minutes.

Nikki woke up from her nap, after a little over 2 hours, refreshed and ready to get to work. As soon as she woke up, she rolled over and picked up her phone to unlock it and begin the journey of surfing and searching for more information. Nothing else was on her mind except the mental replay of the conversation she had earlier with Mr. Ceemore. She refused to stop until she at least got more information about it all.

She unlocked her phone and looked at her home screen with a blank face. There was an urgent message notifying her that one of her favorite vloggers just uploaded an important video. Flixzit allowed content creators to code their video uploads to let their audience know if it was time sensitive or a very important conversation. She accidentally clicked on the notification while trying to swipe it off her screen.

The title of the video scrolled across the bottom of the screen in bold letters: **PASTOR FOUND GUILTY OF SEXUAL ASSAULT AND STEALING FROM THE CHURCH!**

Nikki's eyes widened as she read each word from left to right. Instead of clicking off the video, to do as she planned, she decided to watch it. The reporter was a black woman with long locs and a red dress that had a beautiful A-line that stopped just below her knees.

"Reporting live from WXM, we are covering the story of a well-known pastor here in the city, who was just convicted by a jury of 13 jurors on the rape and murder of 18-year-old Sandlyn Jones and the embezzlement of $200,000 from one of the largest churches in the state," the reporter shared dramatically.

Nikki looked at the screen stunned. She had never met the pastor before, but she knew people who went to the church when she lived in Michigan. This case had been going on for about a year and it had brought a lot of press to the city and the church as a whole, especially with the rise in questionable behavior within the institution.

"Pastor Stevens was found guilty after a week of testimonies, presentation of evidence, and jury deliberation. The victim's parents, family, and friends were present in the court to hear the verdict delivered amongst almost 150 people and reporters. Pastor Stevens denied his involvement to the end of the verdict reading. Although justice was served today, that will never bring back the life of Sandlyn Jones," The reporter stated as she ended her segment.

After the news segment, Lia Marie gave her commentary on the incident and what happened. She began talking about what made her leave the church and her personal experience with a minister. Nikki was unable to finish the video because Lia Marie was getting more personal than she was willing to go at that moment. Nikki decided to call her mom, Della, to chat with her about the verdict. She was sure that she knew someone who knew Pastor Stevens and had some tea to share. Nikki closed down Flixzit, by swiping it off her screen and opened her contacts to her mom's phone number.

ringgggg the phone started ringing shortly after her pressing call. The phone only rang two times before her mom answered the phone.

"Heeeey baby! What's going on?" Nikki's mom answered happily.

"Nothing much, I just finished watching the court case on that Pastor. That was crazy!" Nikki responded.

"Yea Baby, I know. Ms. Jerri was just telling me about how she was surprised he made it this far before getting caught. Apparently, it had been talk at the church for a couple of years that he was talking inappropriately and touching on them young girls at the church. Then to find out he was messing with her for a whole year and then killed her. This world is going to hell for sure," Her Mama added.

"Listen, tell me about it! It's been a lot of crazy stuff going on," Nikki added.

"I know right, that's why I don't even want to talk about it anymore. It upsets me thinking about it," Della stated angrily. "So, what's been going crazy in your world?" she asked.

Nikki laughed, "I thought you just said you don't want to hear anything negative."

"That's everyone else. It has nothing to do with my babies," Della said with confidence.

"Nothing much, outside of getting my business back in line, being a girlfriend and these dreams every night," Nikki responded with a nervous laugh.

"I'm not even going to ask about the relationships. Your business is going to get to where you're trying to get it. You just need to figure out the way to do it and find people to help you. Now, for the dreams. You know I love trying to interpret some dreams," Della exclaimed with a chuckle.

"Yea, it was crazy. In one of them, I had a dream that I saw two women get burnt on a stake. They were slave women who really existed." Nikki jumped in without thinking. As soon as she finished her statement, she questioned how much more she should share with her mom.

"Oh really? Do you remember anything else from the dream? Their name? Colors that stood out? I need all of that if you want me to interpret it for you." She asked.

"Yea, I remember their names," Nikki responded with a short tone.

"Ohhhhh k and what were they?" Della asked sarcastically.

Nikki thought for a moment and decided to only share one of the names. "The name I remember is Rose Sumpter," Nikki said with confidence.

"Rose who? What you say?" Her mom asked confused.

"Rose Sumpter," Nikki answered.

"When I was younger, I remember daddy telling me that his great great grandmother was a slave that was burnt on the stake. I never paid any attention to it," Della started speaking. Her voice started cracking like chicken frying in a skillet, potentially from the thought of her father who had passed over when Nikki was a little girl. Her mom still had a hard time talking about him, even over 20 years later.

"Her name was Rose. His family name was Sumpter until his grandmother married someone and took over the new name. Before her, the family generations had been passed down through males, so they kept the name going. That's how we got to Riles," Della finished her statement.

"What did he say about her?" Nikki asked.

"He said that she had evil in her and they didn't want her to spread her evil to the other slaves. Apparently, she had killed the master's son with the help of her friend. It was so sad to hear that's how our lineage came about," Della answered.

At this point, Nikki was confused. She didn't feel comfortable sharing more with her mom after she mentioned that piece of information about Rose. If this Rose was the same person from her dream, then her legacy had been passed down much differently from what Nikki's dreams and research revealed.

"Oh wow, so maybe we are cursed like you used to say when I was growing up," Nikki said jokingly.

"That's EXACTLY what I meant when I would say that sugar plum," her mom responded.

"Well, I need to get back to this work so I can get to bed at a decent hour," Nikki said to her mom. She wasn't really planning on doing work, but she didn't want to talk any further with her mom on the phone. Her mom had a weird way of drawing information out of her, even if she didn't want to share it with her. It all started back when she was a teenager.

"You sure baby? I didn't hurt your feelings, did I?" Della asked.

"Oh nah, there was nothing for my feelings to get upset about," Nikki responded back nervously.

"Oh, ok baby, I just know you're rushing off the phone. I love you and hope you call me back soon," Della said to Nikki before they ended the call.

"Ok Ma, talk to you later," Nikki said before ending the call.

Nikki spent the next 5 hours researching all of the information she got from Mr. Ceemore. She looked up more information on her alleged grandmothers. She looked up different types of magical powers. She even looked up how to awaken your powers, especially after her levitation experience earlier.

Nikki found herself going down a magical worm hole of information and the seeking of knowledge and understanding. By the end of her internet research, Nikki was convinced that the two women she saw burned at the stake were her great great great great grandmothers. This meant, it was officially time for her to learn where she came from.

All of the signs were pointing to Sookani having truth to her message. There was no way that all of this was a coincidence.

~9~

The Gullam Goochem

Almost a month later, Nikki's DNA results arrived in her email inbox. It was a Monday evening, around 6pm and Nikki was editing a video for Flixzit when the new email notification popped up on her computer screen. As soon as she saw the notification, she stopped what she was doing and ran to her phone. Nikki had been waiting on her results for almost two months, even though they advertised that most people got their results within 3 weeks. She was definitely going to leave a review on that.

A lot had happened in between the time of her talking to Mr. Ceemore and the present. A few days after that day, Nikki started going through severe migraines and insomnia. She found herself always on the phone researching and looking up information on slavery, African countries, and witchcraft. On top of that, her and Torine's relationship was going through a tough spot, especially after the argument they had the night before. During her time of trying to keep up with everything in her life, she found herself becoming more negative, she was crying more, and it was hard for her to sleep.

Nikki went through so many different emotions that she made an appointment with a counselor a couple of weeks ago. She was able to book an appointment with a counselor at the university free of charge, since it was the summer semester, and the school was open. Nikki was taking one class, so that qualified her to receive services. She didn't want to overdo her semester, especially after how hard it was for her to finish her last semester. This was her second appointment scheduled for tomorrow. As Nikki looked at the email, she thought to herself, *maybe this is what I need to start feeling better.*

All of the research had begun to take a toll on her because that was all she cared about. She wanted to find out about her history and float in the air again. But she knew she had to start somewhere, and she felt the answers were in her results. Nikki opened the email to be greeted by a bright red, green, and shiny black banner that read, "Here are your roots!"

Awe, now isn't that welcoming, Nikki thought with a smirk on her face. She couldn't believe she was about to finally find out where she and her ancestors were from. She scrolled down the page, ignoring all the words of the email, until she saw a black button that read: "See your results now!"

Nikki pressed the button immediately and she was taken to a screen with a bright banner scrolling across the screen. The banner read: "Congrats on finding your lineage!"

Nikki looked below the banner and there was a pie graph that was color-coded, with the words "Your DNA story broken down," written next to it. Under that, were the ethnicity estimate breakdowns. Her DNA breakdown was as follows: Nigeria 27%, Mali 21%, Congo 20%, England and Northwestern Europe 12%, Ghana 10%, Benin & Togo 7%, and Portugal 3%.

Nikki looked at the percentage breakdown in amazement. For so many years of her life, she had wondered where her blood came from before slavery. It meant a lot to her to be able to see, in front of her, a look into the countries that her blood has run through. She even had some white in her blood, which was interesting as well. Under the percentage breakdown, there was a section that read: "Your DNA migration."

In this section, it listed 5 community areas where people from Nikki's DNA region typically settled. It was Virginia, East Texas, Arkansas-Louisiana border, Mississippi, and she couldn't believe her eyes with the last one. It stated that her DNA was traced back to the early North Carolina black people. It read that Africans from Ghana, Benin & Togo, and Nigeria were typically brought to that region first, before being moved through the south. What she found very interesting, is that it said many of the North Carolina slaves either escaped and lived with Indigenous people, or they were taken in by Indigenous people when they were freed, as a way to help the former slaves get on their feet. Those who did, adopted the name of Gullam Goochem.

Nikki couldn't believe what she was seeing as she scrolled further on the results list. It stated that they found DNA matches for 20 potential family members. Nikki didn't believe it until she saw a known cousin listed as a person of kin. She couldn't believe how accurate the results were.

She almost texted her cousin out of excitement for the news, but she quickly changed her mind. She realized that calling Tiffany would start a conversation that she wasn't in the mood to moderate. Nikki hadn't talked to any of her family, on that side, since she left after Bibi's death. She was pretty sure there was probably a bet going for who would be the first person to finally reach her.

Nikki scrolled a little further on the screen and stopped abruptly when something caught her eyes. There was a Cynthia and Todd Sumpter listed right after each other. She was assuming they were brother and sister since they were considered 2nd cousins, with a similar DNA match percentage.

Something told Nikki to do a search on Cynthia. It wasn't a coincidence that she had the same last name as a woman she just learned may be her Great Great Great Great Grandmother. From a quick search online, she was able to find a public LookBook page for who she assumed to be the right person. The only reason she felt it may be the right person is because they had 3 mutual friends, who just so happened to be related on her mom's side of the family. Nikki was feeling excited and nervous at the same time, as she thought about the possibility of being united with a distant cousin.

There she was, with smooth milk chocolate colored skin along with eyes that were the color of the Atlantic Ocean. Her hair was curly and laid down to her shoulders. Cynthia was not only black and beautiful, but she also had the mysterious blue eyes. Nikki started feeling slightly insecure because she didn't have the blue eyes.

Nikki started scrolling on Cynthia's page and she found that Todd was Cynthia's twin brother. They lived in North Carolina and it looked like they were very active in their community. She had a lot of posts of her out doing volunteer work. Much of it was with local garden and library initiatives.

Nikki scrolled a little further and something caught her eyes. Cynthia shared an article entitled, *"A look inside the Gullam Goochem language and its historical roots."* With the article, Cynthia added a caption that shared that she was of the Gullam Goochem heritage and loved speaking it with her family and friends.

Nikki felt her body temperature rise as a slight bit of jealousy arose inside of her, the more she read the happiness in Cynthia's post. Cynthia was able to grow up with a knowing of her heritage, while Nikki was in her 30's trying to learn it all like a crash course. She couldn't help but wonder what made her branch of the family tree break off, move, and not pass on history in the blood lineage. What was life like for Cynthia growing up in North Carolina? Was it any different from Michigan?

She sat there with her phone in her hand, contemplating if she should send Cynthia a message to start communicating or not. A large part of her wanted to send a message to start communicating, but she didn't want to sound like a creeper. What should she say? Should she just mention the DNA test and leave everything else out?

Nikki took this time to think about how she would react to different messages being sent to her from a stranger. She wanted to make sure to get her point across, but she also didn't want to appear crazy or desperate.

She sat there looking up at the ceiling, as if she was expecting an answer to fall from the sky or at least into her head. She started wondering about the conversations she had with Sookani. She did say that she would be there when she needed her. Was this a moment when she would call on Sookani to help her? Forget that, how was she supposed to summon her, to even let her know that she needed her? Those instructions were never given to her.

"Sookani! I need to chat with you, pleeeeeeease?!" Nikki yelled out at the top of her lungs. "I need your help; I don't know what I'm supposed to do or say to Cynthia. I am supposed to talk to her, right?" Nikki asked anxiously.

Nikki stood up in the middle of the room with her hands on her hip, awaiting Sookani to appear. She turned around in a slow circle, looking for her to pop-up like she always does. Nikki felt her blood pressure begin to rise as she was getting flustered at her inability to call Sookani. Sookani told her that she would be there as a support to her on the journey, but she was nowhere to be found when Nikki called out to her. That didn't sit well with Nikki and in response, she decided to not reach out or do anything.

Nikki closed out the email browser page and re-opened the tab with her DNA results. Instead of focusing on reaching out, she decided to take a closer look at the information. The DNA results included some information about the Gullam Goochem people, and Nikki was intrigued to find out more information about them. There was a paragraph of information that gave a background of where they came from, which was typically Ghana, Benin & Togo, & Nigeria.

Those of the Gullam Goochem community had a historical background of practicing traditional Kemetac spirituality, intertwined with the Chastianity that was practiced by their captors, and the natural healing practices of the Indigenous people of the land. They are classified as the 2nd largest cultural group among black people on the entire diaspora, with the first being those of the Pelindee who are found in South America.

Nikki remembered learning about the Pelindee people when she traveled to Colombia the year prior. The Pelindee people were the first group of enslaved Africans to escape to freedom and develop their own community, language, and currency exchange. To this day, those of Pelindee still thrive with their own communities and are self-sufficient on themselves for resources. They are said to have a secret town, where only the chosen Masters are allotted the power to see it and enter. These Masters control their self-sustained communities. Only 20% of them speak a language outside of their own language, which makes them even closer as a community.

Nikki started thinking about her visit to Colombia and how beautiful it was to see so many people who looked like her. In the media, they typically showed Colombians who don't identify as being from the African diaspora. The continent has the 2nd largest population of black people, and she was upset at how much she hadn't known prior to that trip.

The Gullam Goochem people apparently believe in a Soul God, who is the keeper of one's soul and life purpose. The Soul God determines if a person is going to have a life of purpose or a life of pain. Only those deemed a pure soul is allowed to enter into the Abundant Covenant. This covenant is said to be made when the baby is around 5 months old outside of the womb. At this time the baby's five senses are activated, and their worldly intentions are being developed until their 1st birthday. It is the belief of the Gullam Goochem people that all babies are innocent until they sign their covenant on their 1st birthday. It's your solar birthday when your soul contract is said to reveal itself to you. At that time, you are presented with two options that determine the rest of your life.

Nikki was reading the descriptions of the Gullam Goochem people in amazement. What stood out most to her, was that she met Sookani face to face on her 32nd birthday. Sookani mentioned to her the need to make a choice, but she couldn't remember the choice she was supposed to make. Was it the choice for her soul contract? Did she choose the right path? Was her 32nd birthday her solar birthday? Is that why Sookani didn't appear when she called for her? So many questions roamed through Nikki's head as she thought about her past communications with Sookani and the new information about the Gullam Goochem. She was hoping that she didn't ruin her soul contract.

Nikki went to her internet browser and started researching the Gullam Goochem people more. She wanted to see what else they were known for and how they fit all of their beliefs into one. Nikki grew up Chastian, so her background was always relevant to the life of being a Chastian. Bibi's husband was a reverend, so Nikki spent many days and evenings at their place of worship. Thinking about how she was taught in the Chastian religion, she was intrigued to see how the Gullam Goochem merged it with the African Kemetac Spirituality and Indigenous practices. This wasn't the first time Nikki saw something about Kemeta and it made her wonder if that's where she should begin her search.

All of a sudden, Reese started barking at the air, next to the bed. Nikki leaned over to see what he was barking at, but she didn't see anything. All she saw was Reese and him barking hysterically.

"Come here baby, what's wrong?" Nikki said to Reese, motioning for him to come closer to her. Reese got up to start walking towards Nikki, but oddly, he walked backwards while still barking at the air. It looked as if a ghost was walking towards him and he was backing away from it. Similar to how he acted when they played with each other.

Nikki was a little worried that Reese saw something that she couldn't see. Her heart started beating crazily which prompted her natural reaction to look around the room. Sookani told her that there were both good and bad magical people and creatures. She started wondering if this was one of those moments where she was going to meet the bad.

Something in Nikki rose up and she said out loud with authority, "Whoever you are, show your face at this instant, I command you!" At that moment, the room started spinning, and a dark cloud formed in the same spot Reese barked at. As it spun around like a cyclops a body started appearing within the dark cloud. First was the legs, then the torso, the arms, the neck, and then the head. It was hard to see the person because the cloud was still taking over much of the visuals around the figure.

"My Dear child, make sure this is what you want to do. Once you open the door, there is no way to close it back," the figure started talking.

Nikki noticed the voice immediately. It was the voice of her Bibi. She hadn't heard her voice since the night before Bibi's death, but her voice was ingrained in Nikki's brain. Nikki smiled and started yelling out how much she missed Bibi and that she loved her. She wanted to talk about everything except what she was just researching, because she was so happy to be talking to Bibi. Nikki hadn't talked to anyone in her family since the incident at the hospital. She didn't know how conversations were going to go and she wasn't trying to figure it out either.

"What do you mean Bibi?" Nikki asked the figure.

"Life, we get to choose the path we want to take. One of beauty or one of pain, it will always be your choice. When the next butterfly lands on you, you will be presented with a choice. One choice will open your access to another part of your brain, that is typically unused brain mass, but it will be hard to manage. The other choice will allow you to live a life of bliss, less responsibility, and a more dependable structure. Once you make your choice, there is no going back," Bibi responded.

Nikki had never heard her Bibi talk in this manner before, so it was interesting to hear. Was Bibi talking about the choice that the Gullam Goochem have to make on their solar birthday? Was Bibi Gullam Goochem too and just didn't tell Nikki? What choice did she make? Nikki was in a state of discombobulation as her brain worked overtime to make sense of everything going on around her. The last conversation she imagined herself having with Bibi would be related to something so estranged from their normal conversations. Bibi never spoke to her about any of those things and neither had her mom. Nikki was beginning to feel like most of her life had been developed from a lie.

Thankfully, her counseling appointment was set for the next day because she felt like she needed it more than ever. It seemed like her life was beginning to shift and change in so many ways. With her being so consumed with this new part of herself, she hadn't been as focused on school and her business. It's like they were both the last things on her mind. On top of that, her and Torine's relationship was becoming more up and down as the time went on.

Torine lost his job shortly after leaving Nikki's home which made his communication become even more rocky after that. He had his moments when he would ignore Nikki for days, hang up on her, and gaslight conversations whenever she would ask him questions. She was afraid that his drinking was increasing which enabled the emotional abuse. If they were talking in the evening, it was a given that he was drinking. She came to learn, if he ever told her that he forgot something, it meant he was drinking. After she started picking up on his ways, he started ignoring her and she started nagging him more in response.

After an accumulation of things, Nikki had become very stressed out over her relationship with

Torine. Their relationship looked nothing like what it did when they first started dating. The man that seemed to be so positive, was turning more negative as the days went on.

Nikki was no longer the person she was in the beginning and neither was he. For some reason, even though they both were clearly upset with each other, neither one of them were open to ending the relationship. They would threaten each other with breaking up, but the next day they would make up and promise each other to make it work.

Even though their relationship was going through a tough time, Nikki would always circle back to the problem being him losing his job. She had faith that life would be different for him by the end of the year and that she would be able to start planning her transition to move closer to him. This situation was nothing different from what she saw people around her go through. She saw it with her parents in their relationships, older family members, and her friends' parents. The only no-no was hitting. She made sure that Torine knew that if he ever put his hands on her, that she would be shooting him in the middle of his forehead. He swore up and down that she was crazy after that.

By this time, it was almost 10pm and Nikki was starting to get tired. She had her counseling appointment in the morning and then she had to do some work for school. She had to finish the manuscript for her residency class to satisfy her summer requirements. At this time, she was ready to be done with school before she dropped out instead. It seemed like everything was going at a slow pace, but she knew she was so close to finishing the requirements that she would be dumb to quit. All she could think about was one day being called Doctor, so she kept pushing.

Nikki proceeded let Reese outside to use the bathroom. She didn't bother putting the leash on him, she just let him run outside to do his business. While she stood at the door, she sent a text to Torine to tell him goodnight.

"Goodnight love, I have an early morning," Nikki texted with a heart emoji at the end of the message.

Not even 60 seconds later, Torine responded to Nikki's text message with a night sky emoji and "Love you baby, night."

When Reese came back into the house, he ran straight to his water bowl and started drinking. Nikki, on the other hand, made her way to the bathroom to brush her teeth and wash her face before bed. As she looked in the mirror, she was drawn to her eyes. She looked at the dark brown irises that sat around her pupils, as they both reflected the light from the vanity mirror onto its own reflection.

"If I had to make a decision, what would I choose?" Nikki asked herself in a low tone, while touching her face with both hands. She looked to the left of her, in the mirror, and stared at the reflection of the purple butterfly portrait hanging on the wall.

"What will the butterfly do when it lands on me?" Nikki asked out loud. *What will I choose?* She thought.

Nikki still hadn't quite figured out what Bibi meant when she said that there was going to come a time when Nikki was going to have to choose between two choices. She didn't understand how it would happen and something told her it was best to not stress over the how and focus on the why and what. Would she be notified of what each choice entailed? Or would she be responsible for the outcome? So many questions were going through her head as she brushed her teeth looking in the mirror.

As she lifted her head up, she began thinking about the common link of the word Kemeta from the letter and from the Gullam Goochem. In the letter that Sookani gave her, it mentioned that the Soul of The World was kept in Kemeta before everything happened. Well, it was in Kemeta, but Inami was the magical city connected to it.

She also found from her research that the Gullam Goochem practiced Kemetac Spirituality. Although she hadn't looked up either one of them, something inside told her to do some research on it. It had to be a reason why it came up more than once and it seemed to be very important for both. If there was a link to more information, then Nikki was open to finding it. She was determined to figure out what was going on with her.

When Nikki finished brushing her teeth and washing her face, she went into her room and started undressing to put on her night clothes. She tossed her clothes toward her laundry basket without paying attention to where it landed, and then opened the top drawer of her dresser to grab her gown. She walked toward the bed as she put the gown on over her head. After noticing that she left her phone in the bathroom, she retrieved it from the bathroom counter and walked back into the room. Before getting in the bed, she grabbed her charger from the nightstand and plugged it into the wall. Her charger was 10ft. long, so it was able to stretch and reach her bed, thankfully.

Nikki opened her browser and searched the words, "what is kemeta?" Thousands of results were returned, but the first one caught her eye. It was titled: "Ancient Egyptia: A brief history." In the sample text, it mentioned that Kemeta was an ancient name for the country of Egyptia. Nikki couldn't believe the words she was reading. This whole time, her knowledge of Egyptia had always been from the context of what she learned in church growing up. She was taught that God's people were enslaved there, and they worshipped gods that weren't of the real God. Nikki was even more intrigued and clicked on the article to read more.

She scanned through the article until she got to the excerpt that mentioned Kemeta. It shared that the definition of Kemeta was, 'black land,' and it was believed to be because it stretched along fertile land due to it being blessed by the Nile River, which is still the longest river in the world. Nikki couldn't help but wonder why the name was changed from Kemeta to Egyptia, especially after it was associated with the word black. She immediately went back to her browser and typed in the search words, "why did kemeta change to egyptia?"

Nikki learned that Kemeta was at odds with the Greeks, who had partnered with surrounding areas, as a way to conquer the land due to its rich soil and assumed magical abilities. Nikki looked at the years and noticed that the Greeks conquered South Kemeta, known as Memphis, in 291 BC. She immediately thought about the letter from Sookani and the dates of Alamander's ruling. She jumped out the bed and went to grab the letter to cross-reference while doing her internet research.

She was getting excited as she immediately jumped back in bed after retrieving the letter. She sat up in the bed crisscrossed at the legs, as she rummaged through the information. Nikki was just tired shortly before she started her internet search, but now she found herself gaining energy with each word she read. She couldn't believe her eyes and what she was seeing. What she couldn't believe most was how this was hiding in front of her face and she hadn't seen it there before. Nikki was also embarrassed by the fact that she didn't know that the city she lived in, was named after the city of Memphis in Egyptia. You would think the pyramid replication located in downtown Memphis would give away the history and its connection. But it didn't.

Out of nowhere, Nikki started to think it was ironic that she lived in Memphis and was researching her roots to a city with the same name, located all the way across the world. Nikki started cross-referencing dates, which revealed that the dates of the Greeks conquering Kemeta and the fire at the library were very close to each other. Were the Greeks responsible for the fires? Were they the ones coming after Alamander and the Soul of the World?

It was after the Greeks conquered Kemeta that they changed the name to Aegyptus which then translated to Egyptia. Just that fast the nation changed, over the course of a few years the Arab nations also came to settle in the area, turning Egyptia into a predominantly Cathramic and

Muslana country. Nikki found herself still questioning what exactly Kemetac Spirituality was. She opened another browser window to begin searching the phrase, "what is kemetac spirituality?"

A lot of results were returned, but there was a video from a black woman on Flixzit that Nikki clicked on to watch. The lady's name was, Divine Goddess Rising, and it looked like she was about 40 years old. She started the conversation by sharing who she was and how happy she was to have us watching her video. This seemed to be a common thing among people on Flixzit, Nikki found herself doing the same thing in her videos, she couldn't help but to give a slight laugh as she waited for the Divine Goddess to begin talking about Kemetac Spirituality.

By the end of the video, Nikki found herself happy she didn't click off the video in the beginning, because Divine Goddess gave a lot of information about Kemetac Spirituality, to the point where Nikki couldn't help but have more questions. She found that Kemetac Spirituality looked at the world from the lens of good and bad. There was a light and dark in everything and everything apparently had an opposite. Not only was there light and dark, but there were different gods and goddesses that showcased different journeys and life lessons to learn from, one of them was called the Laws of Maat, which looked to be similar to the commandments. According to her, each God & Goddess, had a community of witches and wizards they ruled.

This was becoming a lot for Nikki to comprehend and take in at one time. She was having a hard time understanding everything being revealed. What was she supposed to be getting from it all? Nikki looked at the time on her phone and it was already a little after midnight. She had her counseling appointment at 9am, so she made sure she had her alarm set to wake up on time. After setting her alarm she went back to Flixzit and watched more videos surrounding Kemetac Spirituality and Gullam Goochem until she fell asleep.

As soon as she fell asleep, she was back in the same tunnel she visited in her sleep time and time again, but randomly the perimeter around Nikki started shining bright as if she had rays of sunlight around her. Suddenly, Sookani appeared in front of Nikki. She was walking graciously, in a beautiful purple gown that extended to the ground with a footlong train. The sleeves sat on both shoulders and accentuated her clavicle bones that brought out the beauty of her face and shiny grey hair that sprang from her head. She had to have been hundreds of years old, but she had the face of an angel that was no more than a gracious 55.

"Hello, my lovely, you called for me?" Sookani greeted Nikki.

Nikki's confusion was written all over her face.

Sookani added, "When you were trying to figure out if you should reach out to Cynthia, do you remember Love?" she asked.

Nikki remembered at that moment how upset she was that Sookani didn't appear when she called for her.

"Yea, that was hours ago. What happened to you showing up when I needed you?" Nikki asked upset.

"My love you have to be at a state of homeostasis to be able to receive and hear me. Earlier, you were frazzled, nervous, and moving 100 miles an hour. Besides that, do you not realize how much you found out on your own without me? It may not have been as bad as you think," Sookani responded.

Nikki contemplated before responding to what Sookani said and thought about the last of her waking hours. She didn't need to reach out to Cynthia to find out information about her family or the history of the Gullam Goochem. She didn't need Sookani either, all she needed was the internet and determination.

"But what if it's a more serious situation?" Nikki asked, in an attempt to find out what would be considered a good time to call for help.

"I already told you My Love, you have to be in a state of homeostasis. I can't come to you if you are not in a place of stillness," Sookani responded.

"So, that's why I always see you in my dreams?" Nikki asked.

Sookani smiled at Nikki and nodded her head in agreement. "There you go. Besides knowing your power, the most important thing you must learn, is how to listen to your guides. You have to learn how to calm your soul, even in the midst of chaos…. Even when you're awake," she responded to Nikki before turning to walk away.

Nikki walked fast towards her. "No, wait, I didn't get a chance to talk to you about what I found in my search. What does all of this mean? What is my power? How do I find it out?" Nikki asked Sookani without allowing her the chance to answer any of the questions.

"When it's time, it will be time," Sookani said before vanishing from Nikki's eyesight.

~10~

Fatal Encounter

Nikki tossed and turned all night and found it hard to sleep for longer than 10 minutes at a time. One moment, she was dreaming that she was in Egyptia, then in the next she'd be at the hospital looking at Bibi. She would go from there to having sex with Torine. Each dream scene would be short, to the point, and very vivid. Eventually, the sun woke up and Nikki found herself unable to get a full hour of consecutive sleep.

By the time she decided to get out the bed, she looked at her phone and saw it was 8:30am. This meant she had 30 minutes to get showered and dressed in time for her counseling appointment. It was a virtual session, so Nikki didn't have to drive anywhere, which was a good thing.

She hopped out the bed and slipped on her slippers that were laying on the floor beside her bed.

"Come here Reese, let's go outside," Nikki said out loud, while grabbing her robe and wrapping it around her body. As she was walking to the back door, Reese came running from under her bed with her towards the door. He was so excited about going outside that he beat her to the door.

Nikki grabbed his leash, put it on him, and proceeded to let him outside the door. While Reese was outside, Nikki went to the bedroom and picked out a shirt, undies, and a pair of bottoms to put on after her shower. As soon as she finished throwing her pants on the bed, she heard Reese barking. He could be barking for one of two things: because he was ready to come back inside or because he saw a living thing move. She had a strong feeling it was because he was ready to come back inside. The older he got, the less he liked being outside once he finished doing his business.

When Nikki made it to the door, Reese was sitting outside the door, staring. This prompted her to open the door and let him in. She noticed while letting him in, there was a man taking pictures of the apartment buildings. He was looking as if he wanted to take a picture of her building, but she came to the door at the same time his camera was going up. She was suspicious for a moment, and then thought maybe he was viewing the apartments to potentially move in.

I can be so extra sometimes! She thought to herself, with a chuckle, while closing the door and taking the leash off Reese. Reese took off running, as soon as the leash was off. He ran straight to his water bowl and started drinking like he was dehydrated.

Nikki made her way to the bathroom and turned on the shower to the perfect temperature. While the shower water started running, she gathered her clothes and towel and threw them all on the toilet seat. She took off her clothes and let them fall to the floor where she was standing. After pulling back the shower curtains, she stepped in the shower one foot at a time. When she was done cleaning herself, she turned the water off, pulled the curtains back, and grabbed her towel to begin drying off. It took Nikki ten minutes to brush her teeth and get dressed. With 10 minutes left before her counseling appointment, she ran to the kitchen and grabbed an apple and hazelnut spread to eat as a breakfast snack.

She grabbed her laptop off the table before plopping down on the couch and opening it at the same time.

"Talk about perfect timing!" She said, as she looked at the time while opening her internet browser. After logging into the school's website, she browsed to the counseling page to enter her virtual appointment. It was a couple of minutes before the scheduled appointment, so she went and grabbed water to drink while talking.

Her assigned counselor appeared on the screen shortly before the scheduled time. He was a white male and looked as if he was around 45 years old, by the wrinkles under his eyes. His hair was a sandy brown and laid right above his ears. He had glasses with lenses that were shaped like rectangles with a forest green colored frame. The arms of his glasses looked like they were made of wood, which made Nikki randomly think of a tree.

He was located in an office space that looked pretty simple from what Nikki could see. There was a beautiful tall plant sitting in the corner behind him. The walls were a soft baby blue color and there was a quote painted on the wall, that read: "I possess an unlimited amount of power that I haven't even touched yet," from an unknown author.

"Welcome Nikki, how are you doing today?" He asked with a very soft-spoken voice.

"I am doing good, still a little sleepy," Nikki responded with a laugh.

"I can only imagine, I'm right there with you," he responded back with a slight giggle. "Well, it's my goal to not put you to sleep while we are together," he continued with a more upbeat tone. "As you learned from our first meeting last week, I'm one of 3 full-time therapists on staff here at the clinic. We have quite a few student interns who work with clients as well, it just depends on the person's preference. I'm happy that we were able to work together. If at any time you feel uncomfortable or want to stop talking, feel free to let me know. How does that sound?" He asked Nikki.

Looking into the computer screen, Nikki responded back with a quick "yes, that's fine." She was used to the disclaimer lingo that therapists tend to use.

"So, how have you been since our meeting last week?" Dan asked Nikki with his head slightly tilted downward. "You were talking about how you had been feeling stressed out. How are you feeling today, in response to then?" He asked.

Nikki paused for a moment before answering. She wanted to make sure she found the right words to say how she felt, and in a way that he didn't take it wrong.

"I've been a little tired, and I feel disconnected from my family. I haven't talked to anyone since Bibi died and I keep having dreams every night. My relationship is also on the rocks, I just feel like everything is falling apart," Nikki spurted out. As the words came out, she realized that she didn't do a good job of organizing her thoughts into words that didn't make it look like she was going mad. She did a good job of not mentioning the magical shit going on with her, but a part of her felt like she revealed too much. As soon as she finished talking, she felt her body temperature rise and her heartbeat increased as if she was going to cry.

"It sounds like a lot has been happening to you as of late. How long have you been feeling like this?" Dan asked.

"It's been going on since Bibi died a few days before my birthday in March, and recently, it's been starting to bother me as I've been feeling alone." Nikki responded. She couldn't believe the words that were coming out of her mouth as she shared what her heart was feeling. That was the first time she admitted out loud, that she felt lonely.

"I can see how getting through the death of a loved one can be quite difficult when it's new. What was your relationship like with your family before Bibi died?" He asked.

"We weren't really close, but I would go home at random times to see them. Whether it was for a birthday party or holiday, I made it a point to go home," Nikki responded.

"You stated, "go back home," how long have you been living away from home?" Dan asked Nikki.

"I've been gone since I was 18 years old, so I always knew if I wanted to see family I had to go home because they weren't coming to visit me. I'm a single woman with no children. All I have is Reese, my dog, and he is nearing 10 years old," She said sadly.

"How do you feel when you go home?" Dan asked Nikki.

Nikki stopped and thought for a moment before answering his question. She had never shared her thoughts regarding how she felt around her family. No one had ever asked her how she felt until that moment.

"You know, honestly…." Nikki started before pausing. "Sometimes I feel good with my family, a lot of times I feel like I'm always trying to make them feel proud, and most times I feel like no one really understands or like the real me," she started spilling out to Dan.

"Like, even at my graduation party, my family had a big brawl with each other, in the middle of the party. I was so upset, that I left to cool down and not think about what had happened. Don't you know that my grandma gave all of my gifts back to everyone? After she just helped jump my mama? Or how about my dad's side, where I was constantly ostracized for being different, left out of fun activities, talked about behind my back, and lied on? If I ever wanted to see them, I have always had to go visit them. Unless it was a graduation or assumed that something was wrong with me; which didn't happen often," Nikki blurted out loud. Her eyes were starting to swell up with tears.

"That sounds like a lot to go through at a time that is supposed to be an important celebration for you. I heard you speak about a fight on your mom's side of the family, was your dad's side of the family there too, at the party?" He asked.

"Nah, they don't really intermingle with each other. Only time they all come together is at one of my graduation ceremonies. They aren't as wild as my mom's side of the family. That side of the family do all of the drinking, gambling, and partying. My dad's side of the family are very religious. Some would say stuck up, if they weren't a part of the church. I lived with my mom until I was 10 years old and then I moved with my dad until my senior year of high school, when I moved in with Bibi after he kicked me out the house." Nikki responded back to Dan.

"You've mentioned Bibi a few times since we've started talking, are you ok with sharing who Bibi is?" Dan asked in a careful tone.

"Oh, sorry about that. Bibi is my dad's mom. She just didn't like being called grandma. She said it made her feel older than her spirit felt." Nikki responded back with a laugh as she thought about Bibi.

Dan looked at Nikki and nodded his head twice, before responding to her statement.

"What do you mean by your family doesn't understand you?" Dan asked in reference to a statement Nikki made earlier in the conversation.

"I just feel like I can't be myself around them. It's like they expect me to be this perfect person and as soon as I do or say something that doesn't appear to be perfect, they have something negative to say or they choose to disown you altogether," Nikki responded. She felt her heart begin to beat faster, and the first tear fell, as she let out how she was feeling.

"Is there someone in your family that you feel you can talk to?" Dan asked.

Nikki stopped and thought for a moment. As she was thinking, she scanned through each person in her family. As each face scanned through her mind, she found herself taking note of the type of conversations she typically had with each person, how she felt, if they ever stabbed her in the back, etc.

"Feel free to take as much time as you need, to think," Dan added.

"Thank you," she responded. She couldn't believe how long it was taking for her to come up with a response to the question. She talked to her mom whenever she felt herself going into a state of doubt or an anxiety attack. She talked to her dad whenever it was something about business. She talked to her cousin when it was about a relationship and she talked to her siblings when she just wanted to let her hair down and talk about things in the world. It seemed like there was no one person, in her family, that she felt like she could share all of her thoughts with. There were particular topics she talked to each person about but that was the extent each conversation went. No one knew her darkest secrets and fears.

"You know what, now that you asked that question. I think I have always tippy-toed around certain conversations with my family. Even right now, there are things going on that I wish I could talk to them about, but I don't know how they would receive it," Nikki responded back.

As soon as she finished talking, she wished she didn't say the last part. She didn't want Dan to ask her about what she meant, because then she would have to think up a lie in regard to what she was talking about.

Just as she feared, Dan asked, "what's going on right now?"

"Oh nothing, it's just that my relationship is not going as good as it was before," Nikki responded.

"Is that what you would prefer to talk about for the remainder of our appointment?" Dan asked Nikki.

Nikki thought for a moment and realized she didn't want to talk about her family anymore. She also didn't want to talk about her relationship with Torine. All she wanted to do was get to the heart of what was bothering her. She started questioning, if maybe the therapist couldn't really help her? Maybe the help she needed was at the hands of someone who understood the spiritual things she had been experiencing.

"If at any time you don't feel comfortable talking to me, whether because of me being a white man, or you just want someone new. I want you to know that it is ok." Dan added after Nikki paused for an extended time to think.

At this time, Nikki wondered what was going through Dan's mind. It wasn't because he was a white man. Or maybe that did have something to do with it. The more Nikki went back and forth in her head, she realized that she needed to get to the heart of her relationship with her family. When she thought about the problems that were going on in her life, everything related back to family and her upbringing. Especially with everything she has been learning from Sookani, Nikki knew all the answers she needed lied within healing her relationship with her family. But that didn't negate the fact that they hurt her often.

"After today, I realize there is some healing I need to have with my relationship to people in my family. As I was saying everything out loud earlier, I realize that I hold back a lot of what I feel with my family because I'm afraid they won't really accept me. All the memories I have from childhood extend from me being told I couldn't do something. The more I think about it, my life has been feeling like a lie for the most part," Nikki concluded. As she finished her statement, a random sense of calmness came over her. She became more relaxed as if her body was waiting for her to admit that she had family issues.

"You have shared a lot today and I can only imagine how it may have you feeling, apart from what you have shared today. Thank you for trusting me with your feelings," Dan affirmed Nikki.

Nikki looked up at the clock and realized almost 30 minutes had gone by already. She was so focused on the conversation and getting to the heart of what she was feeling, time got away from her. She wished they could have more time together, but on the other hand she didn't want to overwhelm herself with all of the emotions that were running through her at that moment.

"Thank you for listening. By just talking, it gave me a lot to ponder on and think about. Can we do the same day and time next week?" Nikki asked.

Dan laughed and jokingly answered, "Oh you don't waste any time, am I starting to get boring to you?"

"Oh nooooo! I just knew that was coming up next," Nikki responded laughing loudly.

Before getting off the call, Dan did a mental health assessment to make sure Nikki wasn't in a place of wanting to harm herself or anyone else. That became required for counselors to do after a student committed suicide, on campus, after leaving a counseling session a few years back.

They scheduled their next meeting and bid farewell. Nikki didn't know what to do with herself at that time. She didn't know if she should work on some work, study, plan material to record, or call and talk to someone. For the first time in a long time, she didn't know what she wanted to do. She felt lost sitting on the couch, as she looked up at the ceiling.

As soon as she closed her eyes, her phone started ringing. With her phone ringing, it meant it could only be someone that was on her favorites list because her phone was on do not disturb. She ran to grab her phone, to see that it was Torine calling. She was surprised he was calling because they had got into an argument Sunday night, that was damning.

By the time she answered, it was the 3rd ring.

"Hey Baby," Nikki answered with a giddy voice.

"Hey, are you busy?" Torine asked Nikki. He sounded firm, as if he didn't have any emotions in his voice.

"I just finished my counseling session. It went really well. How are you doing?" Nikki asked.

Torine hesitated for a moment, then he started speaking. "You know, I've been doing a lot of thinking about everything that happened Sunday night with us and it had me questioning if we could really work this relationship out. I really want it to work, but with the distance I think it's going to be almost impossible for us to be what we need to be for each other. There are times when we are going to get into it and all we need is a hug to make us feel better. We can't do that if you are 1000 miles away from me," he finished.

Nikki squinted her eyes, as if she was trying to figure out what Torine was trying to say. Was he breaking up with her?

"I know baby, that's why I was planning on moving there next year once I can be more remote with my responsibilities," Nikki responded back, as if she was pleading for him to remember their past discussions.

"Yea, I know that, but that's not right now though," He shot back firmly.

At this point, Nikki was trying to get a read on how Torine was feeling and what he was implying, but she was getting cloudy images. "What are you trying to say? Are you saying you want to break up?" She asked him bluntly.

Torine was quiet for about 5 long seconds before he started responding to Nikki's question. Before he started speaking, Nikki heard him take a deep breath and her heart started beating fast.

"I think maybe right now, with the distance, this isn't the best time for us. Maybe if you were here right now, it would be easier for us to build a life together. But you're not and that's hard for me to look past," Torine said to Nikki. This time, his voice was much lower than when the conversation first started.

"But what if I was there right now?" Nikki asked him. Her voice was cracking, and she was starting to sound afraid of ending the relationship. She still desperately wanted to do whatever she needed to make it work.

Without hesitating to answer, Torine responded, "But you're not, and that's the problem."

There was a long silent pause between them as it seemed like they both were fishing for the right words to say in the moment. Not wanting to break the silence, Nikki took a deep breath and decided to be the one to say something.

"I totally understand, and I wish you the best of luck with everything. I'll talk to you later," Nikki said. She didn't give Torine the opportunity to say anything back before ending the call. She didn't have it in her to hear anything else that felt like bad news.

As soon as she ended the call, her breathing increased, It felt like her heart was beating so fast that it felt like it was jumping out of her chest. She was still in shock of what had just happened. She couldn't believe that Torine decided to break up with her even though they had future plans together. Distance wasn't a problem in the beginning, so it was hard for her to accept it being a problem now. At this time, tears were running down her face.

In that instant, she found her whole body getting numb as the tears fell faster. She could no longer feel. She could no longer understand. She stood there thinking about her man breaking up with her. Nikki knew their relationship was going through a rocky patch, but they were still new, and she thought they were building something stronger.

The more Nikki got upset, the redder she turned. The redder she turned, the hotter her blood temperature rose until she turned into a ball of fire unexpectedly out of nowhere. As the flames consumed her very being, Nikki started turning around in a circle as she looked at herself in amazement and confusion at the same time. Although Nikki's body felt like it was only overheating to the temperature of a mild fever, the flames coming from her body were giving off heat well over 500 degrees Fahrenheit.

Nikki screamed out loud as her body turned into a ball of fire. The more she screamed, the larger the flames on her body got. It was as if her screams were providing fuel to her new armor of fire. Nikki ran to the bathroom, afraid to touch anything, she placed her hand in the toilet to see if the flame would go out. As she waved her hand back and forth, in the toilet bowl water, it started to evaporate.

She panicked even more, confused as to how she became a human ball of fire and what she was supposed to do, to make it stop. She found herself alone in the middle of her apartment, confused on how to extinguish her body of fire. There was no Sookani and there was no Bibi, it was just her left there to figure it out alone.

Nikki started thinking about what Sookani told her she had to do, in order to summon her. Maybe, just maybe, the same way she was supposed to summon Sookani was the same way she could control her fire powers. It was hard for Nikki to calm down from panicking, but that's what she had to do if she wanted to concentrate. She started replaying the conversation she and Sookani had the last time she appeared in her dream. Sookani told her that she had to be at a state of homeostasis for Nikki to summon her. But she only came to her in her dreams? Did that mean the only time Nikki could talk to Sookani was when she was asleep?

No, she said I could do it awake, Nikki remembered.

None of it was making any sense to her at that moment. The next thing she knew, more tears started running down her face as she got more frustrated. As each tear fell, her fire got larger and larger until she lit up the entire room. She was wondering why nothing was burning around her as she raised her hand to examine it. Turning her hand from side to side, Nikki noticed there was a web-like design where her tattoo was once located.

A year prior, Nikki got the number 11:11 tattooed on her left wrist because she had been seeing it daily, whether it was in the morning or the evening. Unfortunately, now the 11:11 was no longer showing, it was now something that looked like a spider web with a blue eye in the center. Nikki noticed the design of the eye from somewhere, but she couldn't think about where, at that moment. In an attempt to keep from getting upset and making the flame grow, she started talking to herself while looking at the spiderweb eye.

She started concentrating to induce her memory of where she had seen the blue eye before. Out of nowhere, the room started spinning and Nikki was laying in someone's arms looking up at a woman. The closer she looked at the woman, the more she realized that the woman resembled a younger version of Bibi.

It was that moment she panicked even more and wondered what perspective she was looking from. She raised her arm and legs to find out she was in the body of a baby. The only thing she had on was a diaper and footies. Bibi was looking down at her smiling and laughing, while tickling Nikki under her arm. Out of nowhere, Nikki started laughing uncontrollably, and she forgot everything she was worrying about prior. As soon as Nikki began kicking her feet in the air, she fell to the floor.

When Nikki's body hit the floor, she realized she was back in her normal body. Instead of being dressed like she was before, she was now naked with nothing on. The only thing that ran through her mind at that moment was her being able to be in Bibi's arms and look into her eyes again. Nikki lifted her wrist to see if the spider web with the blue eye was still there- Unfortunately, it was gone.

For a moment, Nikki had the opportunity to experience bliss by seeing her Bibi and just that fast it was taken from her again. It was intriguing to Nikki how the last time Bibi came to her, she was telling her that she needed to make a choice, but this time Bibi was in a younger body and she had a totally different attitude towards Nikki. Maybe it was because Nikki was a baby or maybe it was because she was embodying fire. Either way, there was no way to tell and that made Nikki miss Bibi even more. Hell, Nikki didn't understand how she turned into a baby in the first place. She had so many thoughts running through her head.

All of a sudden, Nikki got the urge to drive to Michigan. She wanted more time with Bibi and all she wanted to do was be in the presence of her. The only choice she had at that time was to travel and visit Bibi's home and grave. Bibi bought her grave plot almost 10 years prior to her death, so Nikki already knew where she was buried. That was the only way things would be able to make sense in her eyes. She ran into the room and started throwing clothes on the bed from her dresser drawers. She didn't care if the clothes were matching or not, all she cared about was that they were clean. Within 15 minutes, Nikki had a clothes bag, Reese's travel bag, and her clothes on ready to go. She put everything in the car and sped out the parking lot.

She wasn't 2 miles away from her home before she realized that she wasn't thinking clearly and decided to turn back around and go home. When she got home, she let Reese into the house and decided to go get food. Nikki cruised down the main road and made her way toward the interstate, heading to her favorite salad spot. A few miles up the road, she took the exit on the right to merge onto the freeway. The freeway entrance was a deep curve that mirrored the shape of a circle. As she started the curve, she put her foot on the gas and sped up. Something about speeding up the car increased her adrenaline, and she forgot how she was feeling just 20 minutes prior.

All of a sudden, Nikki's car jerked, and she lost control of the steering wheel which forced her car to raise on the right two wheels. Unable to gain control of the car, Nikki's car flipped on its side and hit the side railing of the ramp forcing it to flip on its back. After hitting the rail, the car behind her mustn't have been paying attention because their late reaction to Nikki's car forced them to avoid hitting her one-second too late. Their car scraped the side of Nikki's car before the owner of the car was able to recorrect.

The driver of the car pulled over on the side of the road once they entered the interstate and immediately called 911. By this time, Nikki was left unconscious in a flipped car, as her fate lied in the hands of someone else.

It took almost 5 minutes for the ambulance and police to arrive at the scene of the accident. They immediately started accessing the vehicle to make sure it was safe to approach. One of the EMT's noticed there was a trail of gas leaking from the rear of the car, which meant the situation could turn fatal at any moment. He wanted to tell his co-workers, but he decided to take the risk of getting Nikki out of the car instead. He knew if he said something, they would be directed to not approach the scene.

The team ran to the car and immediately started trying to get the car door jarred open. It took the team about 5 minutes to get the car door open. As soon as they got the car door open, someone notified everyone of a spark that appeared at the rear of the car.

"GET BACK!" the EMT yelled at his coworkers. "It's going to catch fire at any moment!" he screamed.

They all started backing away from the car, leaving Nikki there, still in her seat as the sparks turned into a traveling flame. The man who noticed the gas in the beginning started looking between his left and right before running back to the car. His co-workers yelled at him to stop.

"Nooooo, Daaaave!!! It's going to blow up!" One of his co-workers fearfully yelled.

Dave didn't listen to his co-workers and kept running. The flame at the back of the car was starting to get bigger.

"NOOOOO!" Yelled another co-worker as the gas tank blew up on the car and the fire got bigger after the large explosion.

Nikki suddenly regained consciousness of everything going on, just as Dave was trying to take off her seatbelt. Nikki started trying to help him take the seatbelt off as well, which caused both of them to fumble with it frantically. They both were breathing heavily but, were determined to get her out of the car before it exploded.

"GET AWAY FROM THAT CAR DAVE!" Yelled one of his co-workers now crying.

By this time, traffic was held up on both sides of the interstate and the entrance to the freeway. Some people had got out of their cars to watch everything take place, a lot of them even had their phones out recording every detail. After a few moments of scrambling with the seatbelt, they were able to get Nikki out of it. At that same moment, the back of the car blew up, tossing Dave backwards.

"Nooooooo!" He started screaming as the car went up in flames.

Just as the flames made their way to the front of the car, they mysteriously started to extinguish on their own, as Nikki came crawling out from the smoke that had begun to consume the area. The flames were contained to the back of the car. It was as if the fire was dying on its own and it hadn't touched Nikki. She made it 20 feet from the car before collapsing face down. Two members of the EMT team rushed in to start caring for Nikki after assessing the area and ensuring it wasn't still in apparent danger.

Nikki was passed out for two days in the hospital bed, in a pseudocoma, before they were able to contact relatives for her. They had a hard time finding the next of kin for Nikki due to the safety functions she had on her cell phone. She didn't have her emergency card accessible, so the police had to get an emergency warrant from the phone company to do a mirror connect to Nikki's phone contacts. From here, they were able to call her mom, who then called her sister Symphonee who lived in the surrounding area.

The sun had started going down when Nikki found herself slowly waking up from her coma. She struggled to move her body, but her eyeballs were becoming extremely active as she was looking around the room. After a few moments, she gained control over her mouth and started trying to move her mouth around in an effort to talk. There was a tube in her nose and throat, which had her mouth feeling quite dry as she started coughing.

"Oh, you're finally awake!" Symphonee said as she walked into the room with a plate of food in one hand and bottled water in the other.

Symphonee was Nikki's younger sister on her mom's side of the family. She lived 30 minutes outside of Memphis in a really nice Condo along the Mississippi River. Symphonee was the principal of a local middle school that served students with juvenile records.

"Hey Symph," Nikki said while struggling to get the words out without slurring them too much. "How long have I been here? All I remember is the accident and then I was here," Nikki continued speaking while trying to focus on pronouncing each syllable of her statement.

"It's just a blessing that you are here. The accident was a few days ago, but they were able to get the phone company to unlock your phone and call mama, then she called me, and then I called..."

"Oh my gosh, how are you doing baby?" said a voice from the doorway. "Is she awake Symph?"

Nikki knew that voice from anywhere, it was her grandma. She must've bought an emergency plane ticket to come see her after hearing about the accident.

"Oh baby, I'm glad you are ok. Your dad is on the way, cause he said he was worried. Were you trying to kill yourself baby? That's what the witnesses say they thought happened because you were driving so fast. Why were you driving so fast baby?" Her grandma continued.

Nikki debated telling them about the events that happened leading up to the accident, but she was still having a hard time trying to piece everything together herself. She couldn't remember where she was going, but she remembered having her counseling appointment and she remembered being hurt by Torine breaking up with her. But what led her to be in the car she didn't remember.

"Honestly, I don't remember everything that happened before the accident. I doubt I was trying to kill myself though grandma," Nikki said while still struggling to pronounce her words clearly and rolling her eyes at the same time.

"Well, your daddy is going to be on the way in a couple of days. He asked me to tell him when you woke up so he could buy his plane tickets," she added in while Symphonee took a seat on the couch and grabbed a magazine from the rack next to its arm. She put her feet up as if she was expecting to be there for a while.

"This is a lot. I really appreciate you all coming to check on me," Nikki said while thinking about how many people didn't have loved ones to care for them. It did feel good that they were willing to come care for her, especially with everything she had going on. In that moment, Nikki began to wonder if she manifested the accident.

She started getting vague memories of her counseling appointment that was the morning of her accident and remembered how triggered she had gotten when she thought about her family. How ironic that something would happen, and they were all in one place together shortly after.

"Of course, we would be there for you baby," Her grandma added.

As she finished talking, the nurse came walking into the room with her head down while writing on her clipboard.

"Alrighty, Ms. Riles I'm here to check your vitals again, how has she been..." The nurse started talking before lifting her head to see that Nikki was not only awake, but she had new company with her.

"Well, hello there Ms. Lucky! It's nice to see you awake!" She said excitedly. "How are you feeling? Do you know where you are at?" She began asking.

Nikki started to laugh, "Yes, I know where I am at Ms. Tammy," she responded while taking a glimpse at the nurse's name badge.

"Good, very good," she responded. "Well, we ran some blood tests while you were in your pseudocoma to see how your levels were and if we needed to watch out for anything. We did find a few things that I wanted to talk to you about. Before doing that, are you ok with me sharing this information with your visitors present?" Nurse Tammy asked while looking at Nikki's grandmother and sister.

Nikki did a brief scan between her sister and grandma to decide if she wanted them to be in the room or not. She had no idea of what the nurse had to tell her and the more she thought about it, she was afraid to have them listen to it. All it took was something controversial, and then Nikki would have to find a way to keep her power in decision making. Whenever her grandmother was present, she had no choice but to feel like she was still a little girl.

"Hey granny and Symph, could you step out for a second for us to talk?" Nikki asked them both.

They both looked at each other before collecting their purses and moving towards the door slowly. Before reaching the door, Nikki's grandma said softly, "I'll be right outside the door if you want some support." Nikki could tell it may have been hurting her that she asked her to step out, even though she was a nurse as well. She trusted her grandmother's judgement of medical practices, but a large part of Nikki wanted to make decisions without the influence of someone else telling her what was best for her.

When her grandma and Symphonee made it outside the door, she saw them talking through the glass window. She turned back to the nurse as she awaited the important news.

"So, what is it that you have to tell me?" She asked while turning back to the nurse.

"Well first off, it's all good news from your lab results. We didn't find anything abnormal from your tests and your body scans came back perfect. It is definitely a miracle for you to have endured so much in that car accident, to not even have a scratch on you! We can't even find what caused your pseudocoma, but we are still looking," Nurse Tammy said with excitement.

"Oh, that's really good news! So, does that mean I can leave soon?" Nikki asked while attempting to pull her body up. Even though she didn't break any bones, her arms were quite sore from inactivity for two days.

"So, about that. Yes, you will be approved to leave tomorrow if the rest of your tests continue to come back good today. But there was more that I needed to share with you in regard to your tests," Nurse Tammy continued talking.

Nikki looked up at Nurse Tammy confused. She couldn't imagine what else she would have to say, especially after saying there was no bad news from her tests. So, what could she possibly have to say?

"Uh, and what exactly is that?" Nikki asked with a dumbfounded look.

"There is never a perfect way to say this, because I don't know if you would be happy or not, but when we run tests, it's routine that we run pregnancy tests as well. While running your blood tests, it came back that you are pregnant. With your hormone levels, it is suggested that you are about 2 months pregnant," Nurse Tammy said with a straight face. It looked as if she was trying hard to not look as if she was happy or sad, as she awaited Nikki's reaction.

"Wait, hold up, what did you just say?!" Nikki asked dumbfounded. "But how? I had my period this last month and I haven't been feeling any symptoms," She added while attempting to pull her body up in the bed.

Nurse Tammy quickly moved over to the bedside and placed the clipboard on the ledge before trying to help Nikki sit up on the bed.

"Oh, one moment Hun, I'm going to help you so you don't strain your muscle strength," Nurse Tammy said to Nikki while helping her sit up.

As Nikki turned to aid Nurse Tammy with shifting her body, she got a glimpse of her grandma looking at her from the window. She had a controlled serious look on her face. Nikki had seen that face once before. The last time Nikki saw that face was when she didn't invite her as her date to an awards ceremony. She seemed so disappointed and hurt that she was unable to be a part of something Nikki did. A large part of that disappointment was because she likes to be in the spotlight oftentimes, and it oftentimes got on Nikki's nerves. Her grandmother could preach at you about all the things that are killing your body, while smoking a pack of cigarettes right there in front of you.

Nikki turned back to Nurse Tammy to figure out what was going on.

"The way pregnancy works; a small percentage of women will experience some bleeding that resembles a period. This can sometimes confuse many when they find out they are pregnant after. I know this is a big surprise for you, but I feel God never makes mistakes," Nurse Tammy concluded with her hand on Nikki's shoulders. Before walking out the door, she turned to Nikki, gave her a big smile, and walked out the door. Before walking down, the hall, she turned and said something to Nikki's grandma.

Symphonee walked into the room first. "Girlllll that was really quick what did she have to say?" She asked.

Before Nikki could respond, her Grandma came walking into the room talking. "Baby, did they say when you can go home? How were the tests?" She asked.

Nikki stopped and thought for a moment before answering the questions her grandmother started asking her. "She said I should be able to go home tomorrow. They found my tests were all clear and couldn't figure out why I was in the pseudocoma for so long. Wait, no, she said I should be able to go home tomorrow as long as the rest of the tests come back good." Nikki finished.

Her grandmother walked over to the bedside and placed her hand on Nikki's shoulder. As soon as she placed her hand on her shoulder, Nikki could feel a warm tingling sensation shoot through her body followed by a painful pinch in her chest.

"Baby, I'm sure everything is going to work out just fine for you my love," her grandmother responded.

"So, that means you can get out of this depressing place. Are you going to your house or do you want to go to mine?" Symphonee asked.

Nikki responded back abruptly with a laugh, "Nahhhhh, I'll stick to my own bed, But thank you for the offer though."

~11~

Crossroads

It wasn't until Friday morning when Nikki was released from the hospital. She was expecting to go home the day before on Thursday, but they found a lump on her head that they wanted to run for more brain scans and tests. The tests came back negative for anything dangerous, so she was allowed to go home with someone willing to stay with her as a support.

Nikki's grandmother's plane was scheduled to leave Saturday morning and her father was planning to arrive that afternoon, for the day. He wanted to come and check on Nikki to make sure she was ok before heading out of the country for a business trip. Symphonee, on the other hand, offered for Nikki to stay at her home or she would come visit her when needed. From the sounds of everyone's schedule and Nikki's current assessment for pain- she was sure that she would be ok home alone.

With all of the support offered from everyone, Nikki still found herself upset at what happened with Torine. While they were carrying Nikki's items to Symphonee's car, all she could think about was the pregnancy news she got in the hospital.

Her and Torine didn't use protection when they were
having sex and they definitely didn't take any safety
precautions. Now, here she was, single and pregnant.

As much as she wanted to find a way to tell
him about the pregnancy, she was going back and
forth between telling him, keeping it a secret, and
even potentially terminating the pregnancy. She had
a few friends who had an abortion before, and she
remembered hearing their stories of how they felt
going in to do it and how it affected their health
afterwards. Only one person said they didn't regret
the decision. The more she thought about it, Nikki's
stomach turned over, forcing her to put her hand on
her stomach and crouch over.

"Is everything ok?" Nikki's grandmother asked
while walking over to Nikki and putting her hand on
her back.

"Yes, I'm good, I think I may just be hungry," she
lied.

It took them about 20 minutes to get to
Nikki's house. While she was gone, Symphonee had
been going to her house and taking care of Reese, so
he wouldn't be in the house starving and using the
bathroom all over the place. As soon as she walked
through the door, he came running up to her with his
tail wagging uncontrollably. Luckily, the time he was

home alone wasn't too bad. Apparently, he did his business inside of the bathtub while Nikki was gone. Reese was a smart dog.

"Heeeeeey baby! I missed you tooooo!" Nikki started talking to Reese while petting him on his head and back.

"Baby, what were you doing before your accident?" Her grandmother asked while looking around the house with her nose turned up. She must've been talking about the mess that had been created when Nikki was packing her bag. She didn't tell them exactly what she was doing before her accident, because the last thing she wanted them to do was lecture her and tell her how she was wrong. On top of that, there were dishes in the sink and 3 loads of clean laundry on the couch.

Nikki started thinking back to that day and why she wanted to go home. Out of nowhere, she realized that maybe everything happened for a reason. Maybe her grandma had information on everything Nikki had been researching and learning about.

Grandma Anjelique was married to Nikki's grandfather for 15 years before they divorced, while her mom was a young teenager. She never really gave the full story as to why they broke up, she just used to say they no longer had similar goals. Nikki never asked any other questions about their relationship after that.

"Nikki, did you hear me baby?" Her grandma asked, which caused Nikki to snap out of the daydreaming trance she found herself in.

"Oh yea, sorry Grandma. I was on my way to my friend's house to spend some time with her," Nikki lied.

There was no way for her to check her lie, since her car was now burnt to ashes. All the proof of her clothes and suitcase were gone. Nikki was thankful that she didn't put anything of value in the car with her, because her feelings would be totally different if that was the case. When she returned home to drop Reese off, she put her work bag in the house.

"Oh ok," she responded nonchalantly while still walking through Nikki's house looking around. She was looking like a detective trying to find something, which was slightly alarming to Nikki.

Symphonee interrupted and told them that she was going to go home for a while to relax and freshen up. "I'll be back after I get a little work done. This will give you both some time to spend together before she leaves," Symphonee said to Nikki.

"Alrighty Symph, thank you for all of the help you have been giving me during this time. By the time Grandma leaves, I won't be needing any help," Nikki said giggling. "You still have your key, right? You might as well keep it," she continued.

"Yea, it's in my car. I wasn't planning on giving it back anyways," she added while laughing and grabbing her purse. Before walking out the door, she yelled to the back of the house, "See you a little bit later granny, let me know if you need me to bring anything back with me."

"Alright hun, love you!" Grandma yelled to Symphonee.

They had food left over from what they grabbed to-go, on their way home. So, they didn't really need anything at that time. Nikki was no longer thinking about food. As soon as Symphonee said she was leaving for a while, Nikki thought this would be the perfect time to change the conversation, to see if she could get any answers from her grandma. By the way her Grandmother was looking around her house, she was bound to find something that would make her start asking questions.

"Hey Granny! I have a question for you. Do you mind coming in here and chatting with me?" Nikki yelled to the back room. Part of her reasoning was to create a distraction. Another part, was to see if she could get more information from her.

"Of course hunny," she responded while walking back to the living room and taking a seat on the other couch. "What's going on hunny?" she asked with a voice of concern.

"Lately, I've been having a lot of dreams and messages have been coming to me so clear in regard to history and family," Nikki started talking. "So, I found the name of my Great Great Great Great Grandma Rose from Grandad Ed's side of the family. I asked my mom about her and that's how I found out who she was. Now, I'm finding myself doing more and more research about her and it's becoming a lot," Nikki added with slight excitement in her voice.

Nikki's grandma was looking at her closely as if she was trying to study her emotions and how she was feeling. With her eyes squinted, she asked, "How did you find out about Rose?"

"It honestly all started from one dream and that dream spiraled into more. After that dream, I have been having a lot of out of body experiences and seeing things and people related to the past and history. I even did my DNA test to find information about my family roots and people I haven't met yet," Nikki started running off at the mouth.

"Oh hunny, it sounds like you have been experiencing a lot as of late. Have you changed anything in your life? How is your diet? Have you been taking any medications?" she asked Nikki.

Nikki looked at her confused. It didn't sound like she was really interested in what Nikki was saying to her. "Everything has been fine. I've been eating well, and you already know I do not like taking medication of any kind," Nikki said before pausing for a moment and asking the next question she wanted to ask.

"Did Grandpa Ed ever talk to you about his Grandma Rose?" Nikki asked in a sincere tone.

Nikki's grandma started looking up in the air as if she was thinking or trying to find the answers to the question Nikki asked her. Nikki could tell by her reaction that she had indeed heard of Rose before. What she couldn't figure out, was why she was acting the way she was acting. Just as Nikki began to question her grandmother and the information she was sharing, there was a knock at the door. They both stopped what they were doing and looked at each other before looking at the door.

"I haven't told anyone about what happened and I'm not expecting company- I don't know who that could be," Nikki said. She was looking as if she was going to ignore the door, until her grandmother jumped in and remembered who it may be.

"I think that may be your dad hunny," her grandma said.

"But I thought he wasn't coming until tomorrow?" Nikki asked.

"That's what he told you? Oh my, he messaged me while you were sleeping earlier this morning and said he was on the way to the airport. I'm guessing he must've had a straight flight. I told you he was supposed to be here in a couple of days," She finished.

"Well, a couple of days, typically mean about 2 or 3. He could've been here the first day, but whatever," Nikki said under her breath while rolling her eyes.

Something in Nikki didn't feel right. Why didn't he tell her that he was coming early? The last thing she was prepared for, was having both her dad and grandma in one location at the same time. She hadn't seen or talked to her dad since everything that happened after Bibi's death. So, she didn't know what to expect. On top of that, whenever they were both together, Nikki was back to feeling like she was a little girl again. For some reason, she always felt like she had to ask for permission to be an adult around them. She was never allowed to have an opinion- only if it was a writing prompt for school. For these reasons, she preferred to communicate with one of them at a time.

They both looked at each other, as if they were trying to decide who would be the one to answer the door. After staring at each other up and down, Nikki's grandma made her way to the door to open it. By this time, she could easily tell that Nikki was not very happy about her dad coming to visit earlier than she expected.

"Are you all covered up?" She asked Nikki while headed to the door. "One minute, I'm on my way," she yelled to the door.

When she made it to the door, she unlocked the main door and unlocked the 2nd one after struggling with it for a few moments.

"Whew, this door is slightly hard to handle," She said while opening it to greet Nikki's dad. "Heeeey there Pete! Good seeing you, get on up in this house," Ms. Anjelique greeted him at the door as she patted him on the shoulder."

"Hey, there Ms. Anjelique, it's good to see you! Have you been well?" He asked as he walked through the door, stomping his feet on the front door mat, before giving her a big hug.

"You know, I've been doing well. Dad hasn't been doing too well, but I had to come check on our girl," She responded back to him while looking in Nikki's direction.

Nikki got slightly confused at her saying that her grandfather wasn't doing well. Her grandma hadn't told her that, the entire time she'd been visiting. She almost interrupted their meet and greet but decided to be quiet and ask her grandma later.

"You know what Pete? I can't complain. I see you have been doing really well for yourself and your business! I'm proud of you. I wish more of our black kids would realize that if you want to get anywhere in life, you have to learn how to play the white-man's game. Go to their schools, get their education, get their money, and live a comfortable life," Nikki's

Grandma said before turning to walk back into the living room. "It's as simple as that," she finished before taking a seat.

"I know that's right," he responded while walking behind her. "Hey there baby girl, how are you feeling and holding up?" He asked Nikki.

"I'm doing ok, just a little sore at this point, but I should be ok," She responded while struggling to sit up.

"That's good baby, because we were kind of worried about you and everything," Pete said to Nikki.

Nikki took a deep breath and then replied, "I know, grandma told me that you all thought I was trying to commit suicide." She took another deep breath in and continued talking. "Now, you both know I am not thinking about killing myself."

"Well, why were you driving so fast along the freeway? The people said it looked like you were trying to cause an accident," Pete added in.

"I lost control of my wheel," Nikki responded quickly.

Nikki's Grandmother looked between the both of them and felt it was the perfect time to interject and change the conversation slightly.

"Come on in here and have a seat Pete. Have you eaten anything yet? We have some leftovers from this delicious restaurant we stopped at earlier- or I can cook you up something."

"Oh no Ms. Anjelique, I don't need any of those things. I'm doing just fine. I'm just glad I could make it down between all of these work appointments. I'm supposed to be headed to China in a couple of weeks for my company, to make a big deal, so keep me in your prayers," Her dad responded while taking a seat on the same couch as her grandmother.

"Oh, you know I definitely will," Nikki's Grandma said joyfully.

Nikki's dad immediately looked back her way before shaking his head from side to side. "You know you have to be more careful when driving Nikki, you never know how the roads will be when you are driving," He added.

Nikki started rolling her eyes and talking to herself in her head. *How dare he come in here and start blaming me because I lost control of my wheel?*

Can he just be happy that I'm alive? He's assuming too much and lacking compassion when I honestly need it most. Nikki started thinking to herself.

Instead of responding to her dad, Nikki stayed quiet and laid on the couch as if he wasn't talking to her. As a child, this is something she learned to do with him, eventually he always ended up talking to himself. Although she decided to ignore him, it didn't stop the rage that was starting to build up inside of her.

"Nikki, how are you and that young boy doing? Your mom told me that you were seeing a young man that you came up to see for your birthday when Bibi died," Her grandma asked.

As soon as she asked Nikki that question, Pete's eyes immediately shot towards Nikki and she knew exactly why. This was open season for them to start discussing what happened at the hospital when Bibi died. Pete's eyes started glossing over.

"Well long story short, we are no longer together. He broke up with me the day of my accident," Nikki responded.

"Is that why you tried to kill yourself?" Her grandma asked out of concern.

"I just told y'all that I was not trying to kill myself!" Nikki responded angrily while slightly struggling to pull herself up on the coach. "I swear y'all don't be listening to me when I talk."

They both looked at each other as if they were deciding who was going to respond to Nikki's accusations first. From the looks of it, her grandma caught it first.

"It's not that we don't listen to you, we are just concerned about you and the direction you are going in your life. You are 32 years old and you're still single living in an apartment."

"Not to add in, you can't even afford to keep all of your bills paid with your work. You've been in business for almost a year and you are still stuck in this same place," Her dad added while looking around the living room with a face of disgust.

Nikki became enraged hearing him say those words. She quit her job to go full-time entrepreneur almost a year prior. Unexpectedly, the market had begun to fall, right when the Kurlona disease started ravaging the world- which affected her business. Even though she had over $15k saved up for her transition, it didn't prove to be enough after 6 months. Interestingly enough, her dad was one of the people excited to hear about her going into her business full-time. He would always say he didn't understand how she was able to do so much with work and her other responsibilities.

Little did he know, Nikki was struggling with keeping up work as a teacher, her business, content creation, and school full-time. Her health was going through a decline and she was in and out of the doctors for health problems that stemmed from the stress related to all of her work and responsibilities.

That was something sensitive to Nikki because it was a dark time in her life. She was even considering suicide at one point because everything was so difficult for her to keep up with. From the sounds of it, they preferred she stay in the stressful job market instead of following her passions and what she liked to do. You would think he'd understood her internal desire. Her dad had become a millionaire after a short period of time in business.

Peter continued talking, "On top of that Nikki, it really hurt when you had that episode at the hospital with my brothers because you couldn't get your way."

"What happened at the hospital?" Her grandma asked with her neck extended.

At this time, Nikki was getting upset with how the conversation was going. She felt her blood beginning to boil and all she could think about was them both getting out of her house.

"Oh, Ms. Thang had the nerve to have a blow up fit because we didn't include her with pulling the plug. Her and my brothers got into it and I just let it happen because she was acting really spoiled. Just because Bibi treated her like her daughter, it didn't mean she had the privilege to help make the same decisions that her real sons had," He continued talking.

"Nikki, it sounds like you have a lot that you need to look over in your life. You have been getting bad blood with a lot of people then you had the nerve to tell me that you have started messing with the devil's work," her grandmother added.

This threw Nikki off because she hadn't mentioned anything to her about doing anything related to the devil. Where was she getting this information from?

"What do you mean by the devil granny?" Nikki asked.

"Well, first off, I don't like those videos you put on your Flixzit page. It looks like you sold your soul to the devil with all that lingerie and body talk, then you asked me about Rose, which means you may be dabbling in some things you aren't supposed to be in," She answered Nikki.

"Hold up, how dare you say what I put on my page is selling my soul to the devil, especially when I'm advertising lingerie that is sold by my own sister, your daughter," Nikki said, with a raised voice, while looking at her dad.

"What you both are not going to do, is come into my house after I just had a traumatic accident to berate me for every decision you feel I made in error," Nikki said. As she spoke, her body started turning into the same big flame of fire as the day of her accident. She immediately panicked, because she didn't know what was happening and why. Could they see her changing?

As she looked up from her hands, she noticed that both her grandmother and father had begun changing shape as well. This surprised her, because it meant they too had special powers that she never knew. But why were they changing as well?

Her grandmother's skin turned a bright lime green color and her face slimmed out with a pointed chin. Her skin's imperfections were more noticeable than before as well. She had a mole above the right side of her lip and a large bump on the left side of her nose. Her dad on the other hand, still looked like himself, but his eyes were a dark piercing red.

Nikki was no longer worried about her being a ball of fire and was more concerned about her dad and grandma. Why hadn't she known that they had powers this entire time? Unfortunately, she didn't have enough time to figure it out either.

Out of nowhere, her dad shot a bolt of light from his eyes and they hit Nikki in the chest, forcing her to the ground. They both started walking towards her slowly, as she crawled backwards attempting to get away. She wasn't moving fast enough, because her grandma pointed her finger at Nikki and started raising her body into the air. With her body limp, hanging in the air, her grandmother moved her hand sideways which sent Nikki flying into the wall.

"How dare you get upset with us?! We raised you!" Her grandmother screamed out.

When Nikki's body hit the wall, the power of the blow made the shelf fall over. All of the contents fell over Nikki, hitting her before hitting the ground. Last to fall, was a butterfly knife that her late grandfather gave her when she was a little girl, right before he died. He was really big into fishing, so he kept knives and fishing gear everywhere. When he gave Nikki the knife, he told her that it would end up being her best friend. She didn't know what he meant when he said it, and still didn't in that moment. She only wanted the knife, because it had the word butterfly in it.

Nikki looked at the butterfly knife again and thought about the interaction she had with Bibi. Bibi told her that there would be a time when she would have to make a decision. This must've been that time; she began to think as she picked it up and rolled over to dodge another attack.

When she looked up, both her grandmother and dad were standing over her as if they were preparing to toss her again. Nikki yelled out, "What do you both want from me?!"

"It's time for you to die," Her grandmother screamed before picking her body up again. "You will not rise up against us. We will always know what is best for you!" She continued talking while tossing Nikki into the other wall.

Nikki raised her hand as if she was trying to stop another attack. As she raised her hand, flames started to shoot out of her wrist, hitting her grandmother and forcing her to fall backwards.

"Ohhhh, I see you want to do this the hard way!" Her dad added in, as her grandmother fell back. He looked her way and began shooting through his eyes, barely missing Nikki's body. She ran to the door and outside to get away from them. They both made their way to the door and looked left and right to see which direction Nikki went in.

Her dad scanned the area with his eyes, which enabled him to see Nikki hiding along the side of the building. As soon as Nikki saw their feet getting closer, she started walking backwards and shooting fireballs their way. Her fireballs were able to knock her dad down, briefly, but her grandmother flew in the air and landed behind Nikki. This threw her off guard.

Nikki hadn't noticed her land behind her, which made her an open target. She grabbed Nikki and yelled out the words, "suhi wee juumeh!" All of a sudden, Nikki could no longer move or see anything around her. She was bound by an invisible enchantment that placed a bind around her. She wiggled from side to side in an attempt to break free from the binding spell that was just placed over her. Her heart was beating fast and she felt like she was about to die, the more she struggled.

"Arrrrrrrgh!!!!" Nikki yelled out loud, hoping to gain some form of power she didn't know she had.

"We finally have her! Poor child thought she would be more powerful than us!" Nikki heard her grandmother saying to her dad. She couldn't see where they were at, but she felt like they weren't too far away from her body.

Nikki had to quickly think of something to help her break free from the binding spell. Sookani told her that she was a chosen witch, which meant she should be able to break free. She turned her head, in an attempt to rest and think, and saw the same cat she had saw earlier that year outside her apartment. It was just staring at her, as if it wanted to say something. The cat started walking towards Nikki before saying, "only fire made of anger can ravage the strongest of spells," and turning away.

Something in Nikki told her not to question the cat or even the fact that she just heard a cat speaking to her. *Only anger can break the spell*, she started repeating to herself as she started thinking about all the things that made her angry.

Nikki started thinking about her childhood and different unfortunate moments she encountered from her parents, she thought about Bibi dying, she thought about Torine breaking up with her, and she even thought about her friends who passed away too early. As she thought about each incident, the angrier she got. The angrier she got, the more powerful she became. The more powerful she became, the hotter and brighter her flame became, until it was blue.

"What are you doing?!" She heard her grandmother say in the nearby area.

As Nikki started speaking, she felt the spell breaking from her body. "You will not control me anymore," She said in a deep tone while reaching the highest temperature she had ever felt.

Nikki was so upset, that she was willing to kill anything or anyone around her at that moment. She was a force to be reckoned with.

Nikki's body not only broke free from the curse, but she shot fire all around her, which forced everything within 15 feet of her to catch fire. As the fire released, it knocked both her grandmother and father unconscious. As soon as Nikki finished releasing the fire, she passed out unconscious in the same spot. She just laid there passed out from breaking the curse from her body. She was powerless and her flames were beginning to die out, as she used all of her power to break free. Nikki could feel her body, but she felt lifeless as her mind started spiraling into a dark place. As she was drifting, the mysterious cat appeared next to Nikki and brushed against her body.

Next thing Nikki knew, she was surrounded by fire in a place that resembled the way she always thought hell looked like. There was fire surrounding her and people who were severely disfigured. Many of the people were missing different body parts. Some were missing arms, and some were hopping on one leg. Nikki had a sad feeling while she was there. It felt like nothing was positive and happiness was nowhere to be found within her.

As soon as Nikki turned around, she noticed a woman staring at her from less than 5 feet away. This woman looked nothing like everyone else there. She was beautiful with long golden hair and a red evening gown. The shoulders of the gown had rhinestones going around the top with a medallion sitting in the middle of her chest. The medallion was a forest green color that reflected the fire flames that were burning around her.

"Hello my dear, welcome to your visiting hour, who is it that you'd like to see?" The woman asked Nikki.

Nikki was confused by her question, especially since she didn't ask to be where she was.

"I don't even know where I'm at," Nikki replied.

The woman gave off a giggle before responding. "I knew you looked like you may be new here. This is the Keeper of Lost Souls and I am Guardian Medallah. This is where some spiritual souls come after their life of luxury on earth."

Nikki was still confused by what the woman was telling her. She didn't know how she got there and now she was wondering why she was there. She found herself questioning if she was dead. Out of nowhere, a woman appeared from behind Nikki.

"I believe she is here to see me," the woman said.

Nikki knew that voice from anywhere! It was her Bibi talking! She turned around with the quickness to greet her Bibi, only to find that her face was misconfigured, and she looked nothing like the woman she grew up knowing.

"I know, this isn't how you remember me, but we don't have time to talk about that now. Since you are visiting me, it means you have made it to your point of decision. Do you remember when I told you that you'd have to make a decision when the butterfly hit your shoulder?" Bibi asked Nikki in a gentle voice.

"Yes Bibi, I remember," she responded.

"Well, baby, you were born into a lineage of people with special gifts. Some may call us witches and others look at us like we are demons. Unfortunately, many of the gifted choose to ignore their gifts as a way to inherit the riches of the earth. It's not easy being a bearer of the world when instead you can choose to live oblivious to it all. My Nikki, if you choose to ignore your gifts and allow them to be used wrongly; this is where you will spend eternity after your earthly body dies," Bibi said.

Nikki looked around the area, slightly confused at what Bibi was telling her. "Well, why are you here Bibi? What did you do?" she asked.

"That's a long story for another day, my love. But for right now, you only have another minute of visitation left. You are the heir of my bloodline that is meant to break the curses that have been put on our family. The same curses that had your dad and grandma almost kill you today," Bibi finished with a louder tone.

"Kill me? Almost? I'm not dead?" Nikki asked frantically.

"No baby, when you first unlock your powers against a Warkon, there is no killing you during the first fight. The first fight is the moment when you make the decision to choose your path. The first fight is the hardest because it's usually someone you know," Bibi responded.

Nikki developed a perplexed facial expression before asking her next question. Her eyes squinted and her head turned to the side as she tried to formulate her question properly. "So, are you saying my dad and grandma Anjelique are bad witches? Well, Warkons?" She asked with a slight tremble in her voice.

Bibi started giggling, "Oh no baby. They were definitely possessed tools of the Warkon. Your dad and grandma were born with powers as well, but after their solar birthday they chose to not embrace that side of themselves; just like me," Bibi said with a lower tone. At that point her head was down as if she was ashamed of her past life decisions.

Nikki was confused by what Bibi had said. What did she mean they chose to not embrace that side of themselves? What were they possessed by? Were they going to be coming back? Just as Nikki fixed her lips to respond to Bibi, Bibi had turned around and started walking away.

"Bibi! Bibi! I still have a few questions for you!" Nikki yelled after her.

Bibi kept walking as if she couldn't hear Nikki calling after her.

"Bibi!" Nikki screamed, now with tears streaming down her face. It was like no one around her could hear her as she cried her eyes out.

As soon as Nikki fell down to her knees with her face in her hands, the woman from before, appeared in front of her. She reached her hand down for Nikki to grab it and stand up.

"It's always hard the first time my Love. But that is all the time you have for today, I see you're scheduled to meet with Sookani next; one moment please," The woman said to Nikki before saying some strange words Nikki couldn't understand.

"Placemo trantress enicio," Guardian Medallah said while waving her hand in the air.

All of a sudden everything around Nikki started spinning once again. The room was pitch black with purple glittery and shimmering specs glaring around her. It felt like she was in the middle of a purple disco ball with all the shimmering lights glaring around her.

Boom!!

Nikki fell on the ground and this time; she was in a space that looked like gold heaven. Everything was colorful and outlined in gold, with the bright sun sitting high in the sky. There were 7 buildings in the distance, that were shaped like pyramids. The buildings were the color of gold with rainbow arches, guards standing outside of them, and lined in gold.

Nikki was amazed by the beauty around her and all she could do was look around with amazement. She had never envisioned a place as beautiful as this before. People were flying around her; some were on brooms and some were simply floating in the air on their own. All of a sudden, she remembered seeing that place before, in one of her dreams. The difference this time, was that Nikki felt like she was actually present and not just visiting in a dream where no one noticed her.

"Heeeeey Jim!" She heard someone call out to a man who was walking past.

She couldn't believe her eyes as she looked at all the people and details around her. Just as she was turning around, she saw a creature that resembled a unicorn. This creature stood at least 10 feet tall and had a tail that was the color of a rainbow. What set it apart from a unicorn is the fact that it's facial appearance favored that of a person with eyes that remind you of balls of sunlight. Nikki felt extremely happy as she took in the beautiful space.

Just as she started walking, to explore the new land, she heard another familiar voice behind her.

"You have finally made it Nia! It was a long journey to get you here, but you made it. How was your visit to the Keeper of Lost Souls?" Sookani asked Nikki while walking up to her.

"It was interesting. I got a chance to see my Bibi, but it looked nothing like this!" Nikki said while looking around still stuck in amazement.

Bibi started laughing, "Oh, my child. We all have things that we love and everything that glitters is usually never gold," she added while turning to walk in the other direction.

"Noooo Sookani, where are you going?" Nikki asked while running behind her.

"Do you want to know why you are here or not?" Sookani asked Nikki in a snappy tone.

Nikki continued walking behind her as they passed building after building. It was like a small community town, where everyone knew each other and were very happy. She noticed there weren't any homes. It was all buildings that looked like shops. While walking they passed a wand store, a store advertising brooms, and even a potion ingredient shop. There was an herb dispensary and she even saw a slug shop. It was very interesting to see, and she didn't want to ask any questions.

Sookani turned down an alleyway between an herbal shop and jewelry store. Not 20 feet into the alley, she made another turn until they were at the end of the one-way. Nikki remembered this alley as well, but it felt different from before. It also included more than it had in her dream.

"Soooo, what are we supposed to do now?" Nikki asked out of impatience.

"Oh, my dear child, you are going to have a time here I see. Well, that's if you choose to stay or not," Sookani responded, before turning back to the wall.

She raised both her hands to the wall, with them about 12 inches apart from each other. She placed both of them on the wall and stated the words, "I am because we are." As soon as she finished speaking, she stood back from the wall and it started opening. The wall started scaling upwards slowly, with the opening to a dark tunnel.

Sookani entered the tunnel and motioned for Nikki to follow behind her. As Nikki walked behind her, she realized that she had been in this tunnel before. This was the same tunnel she had visited many times before in her dreams. Just as she saw the light before, that same light was present in the space.

They walked for about 20 feet, until the light was the size of a quarter. Sookani whispered some words under her breathe that Nikki was unable to make out. All of a sudden, the light began to widen and got bigger and bigger until the entire room lit up. When Nikki looked up at the ceiling, she noticed that it matched the night sky's constellations with stars and the moon. It was beautiful! Not only did it look like the night sky, but there were also butterflies fluttering around.

Sookani turned to Nikki with a serious face and started speaking, "Nia, the time has come for you to make a decision. You have had the chance to meet the Keeper of Lost Souls and now you are in The Land of Guardians, also known as Inami. This is where people with spiritual powers come to learn their history, how to use their powers, and are trained for their personal assignments."

Nikki looked at her, awaiting her to continue talking.

"Those 7 pyramids you saw are all considered home to the finest witches and wizards of the world. They all came to the Inami Academy of Witchcraft and Spirituality at their predetermined ages to begin their studies," Sookani continued. "The Inami Academy of Witchcraft and Spirituality has raised some powerful witches and wizards that you may know very well from around the world. Well, they weren't *known* to you, but they were very active in our world. We have trained some of the finest athletes, musicians, doctors, and teachers for starters." Sookani continued with a grin of pride on her face. "We are not the only school, but we are the school that your bloodline has a direct connection to. Don't worry too much about that right now though. I'll save the rest for your intro course," Sookani laughed.

"If I stay here, what happens to my regular life?" Nikki asked.

"It will still be there, but it will be nothing like you may remember it to be. You'd spend your time here in increments of 3 months, called trippaths, with 1-month breaks. Your first trippath is intense; the life you had will no longer be," Sookani answered.

Nikki didn't know what to think after hearing more about the Land of Guardians and how life would be different for her. It sounded a lot like college semesters, but without the communication of life prior. She was nervous, but excited at the same time to see how the experience would be for her. Just as she was about to say yes, she remembered the news she received at the hospital. How would she be able to do it all, as a pregnant woman. What would that look like for her child?

"Is everything ok, my darling?" Sookani asked Nikki.

"Yes, sorry, it's just a lot to take in. Is there a way for me to take some time to make a final decision? It's just so much to think about." Nikki responded.

"Is it something you want to talk about?" Sookani asked, with a worried look on her face.

"Not right now. I'm just so excited about everything that has been happening and that's leaving me with so many thoughts in regard to moving forward," Nikki responded.

"Very well, how much time are you requesting? Your trippath begins two weeks from today," Sookani responded.

"48-hours would be perfect!" Nikki responded. That would give her time to talk to Torine and decide what she was going to do with her newfound responsibilities.

"As is above, is also below. Take your time, and I will see you soon my love. You have done such a great job leading up to today and you deserve a break," Sookani said.

Just as Sookani finished her statement, Nikki noticed the room started spinning again and she was back in the spinning vortex. This time, she was spinning faster than she normally would when those dreams took place. Her body was flipping upside down as she was falling down a never-ending hole until, BOOM!

She fell on the ground super hard. It was so hard that her head was spinning which caused her to lay there with her eyes closed until the spinning stopped. As soon as the spinning stopped, she opened her eyes and got up.

About the Author

Moe Nicole recalls dreaming and creating magical worlds from the time she was a young girl. Writing was always her escape away from the real world. Whether in the form of poetry, song lyrics, or short stories- there was never a shortage of thoughts and ideas she had to write down.

The Nia Bluu series is held close to Moe's heart, as many of the inner problems she must face, relates to experiences Moe has had to conquer, intertwined with experiences others can relate to as well. Moe is a full-time entrepreneur and content creator, who's only goal is to encourage and motivate others to live their lives boldly out loud!

This is Moe's 1st book in the series, and she is excited for the other books coming after! Be sure to check out Moe's other work at www.MoeNicole.com.

Acknowledgements

I would like to say thank you to everyone who has grown to love and accept me with all the weird quirks. Over the course of me writing this book, I went into a deep hermit mode where I limited my communication with others. It was needed to heighten my awareness of self and the world around me.

In that time, I was also led to my village. Thank you to those who don't see me as a devil worshipper when I talk about witchcraft. I'd also like to say thank you to everyone who spoke life into this project when I told them the idea. It was your support and enthusiasm that reminded me of my why.

It's important we show more black women leading roles in the magical and suspense world. Thank you for inviting Nia Bluu into your life to fill that role.